Matt's voice w...
we more than g...

'If we were just good ... ...
matter that our lives were so complicated or
that we only got to see each other when there
were other people around, would it?'

'I did warn you.' Matt's voice tickled Tori's
ear. 'I knew it was quite likely I'd fall in love
with you.'

'But I didn't think I'd fall in love with you.'
Tori twisted in Matt's arms so she could see
his face properly. Could touch it again. 'This
is a disaster, Matt.'

But Matt's expression looked anything but
dismayed. 'Are you saying you're in love with
me?' He seemed to get the answer he wanted
from her touch, and turned his head to press a
kiss into her palm.

Dear Reader

Teenagers seem to be experts in creating conflict, don't they? And sometimes it is for no reason other than trying to assert their own independence. I am well aware that even living with one's own dearly loved teen can be a fraught business, and I've done my research on a daily basis for some time now! How much more difficult would it be to live with someone else's teen? Especially for someone who has good reason to vow never to contemplate trying?

Tori grew up with the repercussions of extending a family to include unrelated children. Some were happy—such as the relationship with her foster sister, Sarah (A MOTHER FOR HIS FAMILY)—but others were much less happy and contribute to the issues facing Tori and Matt in this story. I enjoyed exploring those issues. I enjoyed the resolution even more. Hope you do, too.

Happy reading!

Alison

A NURSE'S SEARCH AND RESCUE

BY
ALISON ROBERTS

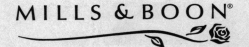

MILLS & BOON®

MILLS & BOON and MILLS & BOON with the Rose Device are registered trademarks of the publisher.

First published in Great Britain 2005
Harlequin Mills & Boon Limited,
Eton House, 18-24 Paradise Road, Richmond, Surrey TW9 1SR

© Alison Roberts 2005

ISBN 0 263 84328 9

Set in Times Roman 10½ on 12 pt.
03-0905-47429

Printed and bound in Spain
by Litografía Rosés, S.A., Barcelona

CHAPTER ONE

'OH...MY *God*!'

Victoria Preston had, as usual, timed her journey carefully to avoid the kind of traffic hassles commuters around Auckland, New Zealand were having to face these days.

This scene of total chaos was the last thing she had expected to see on her way to work.

This was no traffic hassle.

This was a disaster!

It must have happened only seconds ago, while Tori had been singing—no, shouting happily—along with the song rattling the windows of her ancient VW Beetle, just before she'd rounded the bend onto the downhill stretch that led to the bridge across the river.

Another car was pulling to a halt on the other side of the bridge, but Tori was officially the first on the scene as she killed the engine on her car and leapt out.

And what a scene!

A logging truck lay twisted across the road, blocking the narrow bridge. The driver's cab had smashed through the concrete side of the bridge and now hung sideways in mid-air, one giant wheel still spinning slowly. Tori could see the bloodstained, starburst pattern of cracks in the windscreen and a figure slumped over the oversized steering-wheel. The only thing holding the cab above the water, a good twenty metres below, was the twisted coupling holding the cab to a platform now only half-full of huge logs of wood.

5

The spilt logs had done serious damage to the car the truck must have been trying to avoid hitting as it had come off the one-lane bridge. One had also taken out a minibus, which had presumably been travelling behind the car. The van-style bus lay tipped on an angle to one side, with the weight of a massive tree trunk crushing its side doors.

Tori could see a face in the driver's compartment of the van. It was the face of a young child and the sound of screaming suddenly cut through the stunned silence that had been the ominous background during the few seconds it had taken Tori to size up the situation and realise the magnitude of this disaster.

'I've called an ambulance.' The shout from the bridge on the other side of the logging truck was barely audible. 'How does it look from your side?'

'Not good.' Tori was moving towards the minibus. 'Call the emergency services again. Tell them it's a multi-casualty incident.'

'How many people?'

'Don't know yet,' Tori shouted back. 'I'm about to find out.'

The child in the van was screaming too loudly to hear Tori. She could see a woman in the driver's seat, her face covered in blood, moving her arms feebly. At least she was moving, which was more than the driver of the logging truck appeared to be. Another child could be seen, huddled in the gap between the two front seats. He or she was crying, adding to the muted sounds of distress coming from within the vehicle, but that child, too, was clearly breathing adequately.

Tori couldn't see any further into the rear of the minibus. So far she had counted four patients, two of whom were seriously injured. How many more people were trapped in the back of the van? And there was yet another vehicle involved in this crash.

'I'll be back in a minute!' Tori tapped on the intact windscreen of the van and the child in the front stared in wide-eyed terror. 'You'll be all right, sweetheart. Just hang on for a bit. I'll be back.'

This was so hard, leaving the child with such inadequate reassurance and then disappearing from view. This never happened when she was on duty as a triage nurse in the emergency department of the Royal North Shore hospital where she worked. Patients came in neatly packaged on stretchers, with an ambulance officer who could tell her how seriously injured they were. Details of the worst cases would have been radioed through *en route*, in fact, and the trauma room would have been set up with a whole medical team ready to receive the injured.

This was the front line. A place Tori had never been. Thank goodness she had attended that introductory Urban Search and Rescue course last year. Even the most basic procedures for dealing with a multi-casualty incident were helpful and still fresh enough to be pulled from her brain despite the horror of the situation.

She had to see as many of the people involved as she could. A thirty-second evaluation to determine priority of treatment. Airway, breathing and circulation. Disruption to any of those three were the immediately life-threatening scenarios.

For the purposes of triage, she could take the few seconds needed to open an airway and determine whether someone was breathing, and if they were bleeding badly she could apply a pressure bandage of some sort, but that was about it. She had to find out how many victims there were and what condition they were all in.

If there was any immediate and obvious danger to the victims, she would have to try and move them regardless of their injuries, but Tori couldn't see anything too alarming. There were no power lines down, the remaining logs on the back of the truck didn't look like they were going to roll off and she thought the puddle of fluid on the road was water from a crushed radiator rather than fuel with its inherent fire risk.

The children she had seen in the van were breathing well enough to be able to cry. The woman had been conscious enough to be moving. Another glance towards the cab of the logging truck showed the driver to be in exactly the same position as the last time Tori had looked, but even if he was slumped enough to be occluding his airway, there was no way Tori could get into the cab to help.

She could get to the final vehicle involved. A middle-aged man was unconscious in the passenger seat, still held by his safety belt, his head slumped forward. The passenger door was too damaged to open and the driver's side airbag had deployed and now lay dangling from the steering-wheel like a pricked balloon. A woman sat violently shaking in front of it—a horrible, keening moan issuing from her lips.

Tori was trying to open the back door of this car when another vehicle screeched to a halt. And then another.

'Has someone called for an ambulance?'

'They're on their way.' Tori eyed the solidly built young man with relief. 'Could you help me get this door open, please?'

The first attempt failed. Then the man put his foot

against the back of the car as he wrenched at the handle. The door opened slowly to the halfway point with a groan and rasp of uncooperative metal.

'What can I do?' A woman rushed up to the car.

Tori had to think fast. She had been about to climb into the back seat of this car and position the man's head to open his airway and protect his cervical spine, but that would immobilise her and there could be others that needed the expertise she had until the ambulance crew arrived.

'Climb into the back seat,' she told the woman. 'I want you to put a hand on each side of this man's head and tilt it backwards until it's upright against the headrest.'

'You can't do that!' The young man who had opened the door sounded horrified. 'I've done a first-aid course. You can't move his neck.. he might have broken it.'

'At the moment, he's blocking off his airway,' Tori explained. 'He'll die within minutes if it's not opened.'

The woman had squeezed into the back seat. She reached for the victim's head. 'Like this?' she asked anxiously.

'That's great,' Tori confirmed. She could see the man's chest through the window and it was expanding. 'He's breathing properly now. You'll need to stay like that and hold his head in that neutral position until the ambulance gets here and he can get a collar put on to protect his neck. OK? Can you do that?'

The woman nodded but cast a nervous look towards the driver of the car, who was still moaning incoherently. She seemed unaware of the activity around her and was fumbling with the catch of her safety belt but seemed unable to open it. Tori couldn't see any sign of major bleeding.

'Talk to her,' she instructed the head-holder. 'Try and reassure her as much as you can and encourage her to stay as still as possible. Help should arrive very soon. And I'll be back as quickly as I can.'

She straightened to meet the challenging gaze of the young man.

'Where are you going?' he demanded.

'There are people in that van. I need to triage them—check how badly injured they are.'

The man frowned. 'What, are you a doctor or something?'

'I'm an emergency department nurse.' Tori could see a look of relief washing over his face and hoped it was justified. She had just put herself in charge of this situation. Taken control of the scene. This person was ready to help rather than argue. 'My name's Tori,' she continued. 'What's yours?'

'Roger.'

'Come with me, Roger,' Tori said. 'We might be able to break a window or something and get the children out of that bus.'

More vehicles were stopping now. In fact, blocked traffic was starting to build up and Tori shouted to a new arrival to watch that people didn't block access for emergency service vehicles. To her surprise, the man turned immediately to do as she'd requested and her confidence, as she and Roger approached the van, increased steadily.

There was no easy way to gain access to the interior of this vehicle. The log lay over both the bottom of the front passenger door and across the side opening door in the back section. The rear of the van had been crushed by the weight of the log.

Tori caught the gaze of the white-faced child as she

approached the minibus again. She had been away for only a matter of minutes and the girl, who looked to be about eight or nine years old, had clearly calmed down enough to watch for her return. Maybe the reassurance Tori had given hadn't been so inadequate after all.

'We could break the windscreen,' Roger suggested. 'And lift the kid out that way.'

Tori peered through the glass, shaking her head. 'The glass would go all over the driver and she looks injured enough as it is.'

The woman lying half-crumpled under the steering-wheel appeared to be unconscious but Tori could see some chest-wall movement so she was still breathing. Rapidly. A nasty laceration on the side of her face was still bleeding heavily so urgent medical attention was needed here. The wail of a siren, possibly two, could be heard in the distance now, but Tori wasn't going to wait for further assistance if there was something she could do to save a life now.

'What's your name?' she called to the girl, still strapped into the front passenger seat despite the 45-degree angle the vehicle was in.

'Chloe.' The response was surprisingly audible and it was then that Tori noticed the gap at the top of the side passenger window.

She moved to the side of the van and stood on tiptoe to get her mouth closer to the gap.

'Are you hurt, Chloe?'

'My arm hurts.'

Tori could see the distorted shape of the child's left arm, obviously fractured midway between her wrist and elbow.

'Does it hurt to breathe?'

'No.'

'Is your neck sore?'

'No.'

'Does anything else hurt, darling?'

'I don't know.' Chloe started sobbing. 'I want to get out. Mummy's hurt, too. Her face is bleeding.'

'We're going to help you all get out,' Tori promised. 'Who else is in there with you and Mummy?'

'There's Jack. He's hurt his leg. And Toby's asleep and Holly was crying but she's stopped now.'

'Are you the oldest, Chloe?'

'Ye—es.'

The response was a frightened whimper and Tori's heart sank. There were three more children in the back of this van and 'asleep' or 'quiet' could well mean unconscious—or worse.

'I need you to help me if you can, sweetheart.' Tori kept her tone as encouraging as she could. 'I want you to use your arm that isn't sore and see if you can turn the handle to wind this window down.' She turned to Roger, who was staring in horrified fascination at the injured driver. 'Can you try and push the window down to help Chloe open it?'

He seemed relieved to have the distraction of something to do. 'Sure.'

Sirens could still be heard in the distance but they had been switched off in the two emergency vehicles now arriving on scene. The first was a police car and the second a fire engine. Tori saw some of the gathering crowd of onlookers pointing in her direction and then a police officer moved swiftly towards her.

'I'm told you're a nurse and you've got a handle on how many injured here.'

Tori nodded. 'There's a total of eight victims as far

as I can make out. At least two are seriously injured—status two. The driver in the van here and the passenger in that car there.' She glanced towards the cab of the logging truck again. 'Possibly a status zero in the truck and there are several children in the back of this van that I haven't been able to assess yet. How far away is an ambulance?'

'ETA of about three minutes.'

A fire officer was approaching now. Roger had pushed the window of the van right down and Chloe was calling.

'I want to get out! Please, get me out now.'

'Shall I lift her out?' Roger directed the question at Tori but she looked towards the fire officer. Control of any scene had to be handed on to the most qualified person available.

'Is she injured?' the fire officer asked.

'As far as I can tell, her only injury is a broken arm. We need to get her out to have any chance of reaching Chloe's mother quickly—and the other children in the back.'

'I'll get her, then.' The fire officer was both taller and broader than Roger. He was remarkably gentle as he eased Chloe through the gap.

'Roger, can you look after Chloe?' Tori asked. 'Take her over to the side of the road and take care of her until an ambulance gets here.' She turned to the fire officer. 'Can you help me get to the driver? She needs help urgently.'

More fire officers were approaching. A tarpaulin was being laid on the ground and cutting equipment being set up. The police officer was using his radio, relaying the information Tori had given him and requesting further back-up, like heavy machinery to deal with the logging truck and traffic control for the approaches to both sides of the bridge.

The first ambulance pulled up and an officer got out, took a look around at the scene and then approached Tori's group.

'This woman's a nurse,' the fire officer informed the paramedic. 'She'll fill you in.'

The paramedic turned towards Tori and his eyebrows rose sharply.

'Tori!'

'Hi, Matt.' Tori's smile was a mixture of relief and surprise. 'I haven't seen you for ages.'

'I've been on the south side of town.' This was no time to renew an acquaintance, however. 'Have you triaged the scene?'

'As far as I can. We're just trying to get access to the back of this van. There's three children I haven't seen yet.' Tori took a deep breath. 'The driver of the logging truck hasn't moved since I arrived. Possibly status zero. The car over there…' Tori pointed across the road '…has a passenger who's status two, unconscious. His airway was occluded and I've got someone holding his head and keeping the airway patent now. Driver is possibly status three. She was conscious and breathing well but her GCS is down. She wasn't responsive enough to question.'

Tori could see Matt's partner spreading a blanket on the ground nearby and setting up equipment. 'The driver of this van is a priority. She was moving when I first saw her but she's not now. She's still breathing but she's losing blood pretty fast from a head wound.'

Matt had been watching Tori intently as he'd listened. Now he turned to his partner.

'Joe, get a collar and some oxygen over to the other

car and check the status of those patients. I'll stay here and get Tori to help me.' He turned to the fire officer. 'How soon can we get access to the back of the van?'

'We're just checking the stability of that log. We don't want it shifting when we start cutting.'

'Is it stable right now?' Receiving an affirmative nod, Matt turned to Tori. 'Could you grab a dressing and bandage, a C-collar and an oxygen cylinder and mask from that blanket? I'm going to see if I can get far enough through the window to reach the driver.'

Following instructions from someone who knew what he was doing on the front line was a relief. Matthew Buchanan was more than just a paramedic. His training and involvement with the Urban Search and Rescue task force meant that he was an expert in handling a major incident.

Feeling like she was part of a team that was going to deal with whatever trauma this disaster had left in its wake was suddenly exciting. The adrenaline buzz was still increasing as Tori lugged the requested equipment closer, stepping over the hoses from the hydraulic cutting gear. Another child, a boy this time, was being lifted by Matt from the window of the van.

A glance towards the side of the road showed Roger, holding Chloe in his arms. It also showed the arrival of a second ambulance, whose crew went straight to the second vehicle on Joe's signal. Flashing lights from police cars were on both sides of the bridge now and another fire engine was crawling past the traffic build-up. Spectators were being herded further away from the scene, but even with the burgeoning number of emergency service personnel Tori was not asked to step aside.

Instead, she found herself drawn even deeper into the rescue effort.

'I'm too big to get far enough through this window to be in a position to do anything useful,' Matt told her. 'And the fire boys want to try cutting the back of the van first to get in to the other children. There's a baby in a car seat and a toddler who appears to be unconscious. Are you OK to stay and help?'

'I'm not going anywhere in a hurry.' Tori's smile was rueful as she waved at her VW Beetle, now completely hemmed in by a fire engine and two police cars. 'What can I do to help?'

'How would you feel about hanging upside down for a while?'

Tori's level of circulating adrenaline went up another notch. 'What do you want me to do?'

'Get a collar on if possible. Assess her breathing and put some oxygen on. Get a dressing and some pressure on that head wound before she loses any more blood. Maybe start an IV.'

'Sure.'

Tori used one end of the log to gain enough height to get through the open window. Matt passed her the pieces of gear she needed. She was perfectly capable of doing any of the requested procedures more than competently in the emergency department. She had done them hundreds of times.

She had never tried to do any of them whilst hanging virtually upside down over a crumpled door, with her head pounding from the build-up of blood and at an angle that was only secure thanks to the fireman hanging on to her legs.

The woman's airway was patent, the movement of her chest appeared normal and Tori could feel a radial pulse that indicated her blood pressure was not dangerously low, but she was unresponsive. Tori eased the moulded collar into place and secured the Velcro straps. She inserted a plastic OP airway into their patient's mouth and then she took the oxygen mask dangling by its tubing in mid-air beside her and positioned it over the woman's nose and mouth, pulling the elastic strap over the back of her head. She covered the laceration with a thick dressing and wound the bandage to hold it tightly in place.

The van rocked slightly as she was securing the bandage and Tori felt the grip on her legs tighten.

'It's OK,' the fire officer called. 'They're just cutting into the back.'

Matt's voice was also close. 'I've got the IV gear ready, Tori. Sam here is going to pass it in to you. I'm going to check on the other children.'

'OK.' Tori reached a hand up behind her. 'Can I have a tourniquet, please, Sam?'

Her head was more than pounding by the time she had tied the tourniquet around the woman's arm and used an alcohol swab to clean the area above the vein showing in the crook of her elbow. Black spots were appearing in her vision, which didn't help as she slid a cannula into the vein and screwed a luer plug onto the end.

'I need the tubing for the IV fluids now, Sam,' she called. 'You'll need to poke the blue spike into the bag and then hold it up.'

Even her fingers were feeling clumsy by the time Tori got the IV fluids running. If she didn't change her position soon, she would probably faint.

'Pull me out, Sam,' she called. 'I need to stand up for a bit.'

She caught a glimpse of Matt bent over a baby's car seat—his stethoscope in his ears—through the gap between the front seats, but standing up was a mistake. The sudden change in posture after being upside down for so long made her feel extremely unwell. Her vision went completely black and she could feel her legs crumpling. An ungainly collapse to the ground was prevented only by the strong grip on her arms.

'Are you all right?'

'Bit…dizzy…' Tori managed.

'Sit down. Put your head between your knees and take a few deep breaths.'

The buzzing sound receded and Tori blinked to find it was Matt's hand circling her wrist as he took her pulse.

'I'm OK,' she told him. 'I'm just not used to working upside down.'

'You've done brilliantly,' Matt told her. He smiled. 'Thanks.'

'How are the other children?'

'The toddler seems to be OK. He was conscious—just too frightened to move. The baby's had a bump on her head, which may be more serious. They're both being transported, priority one. We're going to break the windscreen and do a dash roll to get the mother out now.'

'And the others?'

'They're being loaded now. The driver's OK—badly shaken but no more than a few bumps and bruises, thanks to the airbag. Her husband regained consciousness but had to be sedated. He was very combative due to his head injury.'

Matt glanced up as a fire officer stepped over Tori's

legs. 'I need you to move a bit so we can get on with this extrication. You feel OK to stand up?'

'Sure.' But Tori was grateful for the assistance Matt gave her and she staggered slightly before stopping to lean against the side of the closest fire engine from where she could watch as they cut open the front of the van and used a backboard to secure and move the unconscious woman.

A new ambulance crew was ready to transport the patient and Tori wondered just how many vehicles had been deployed to this scene. The closest emergency department would be that of the Royal, where Tori worked, and that thought made her glance at her watch and groan. They would be hard-pressed to deal with the influx of casualties and she should have been at work over an hour ago.

'Excuse me,' she called to the ambulance officer on the end of the woman's stretcher. 'Are you going to the Royal?'

'It's the closest hospital.' The female paramedic nodded. 'They're working under a disaster management code for this.'

'I'm Victoria Preston,' Tori told her. 'I'm supposed to be on duty in the ED. If you get a chance, can you let someone know why I'm held up?'

'Sure.'

'Do you want to go with them?' Matt had overheard the interchange. 'The police can arrange for your car to be sorted later.'

'Are you leaving now?'

Matt shook his head. 'We're on standby for the moment in case anyone gets injured, trying to clear this scene. The crane's arriving now, too, so we'll wait until we can check the truck driver. Not that I hold out much hope for him.'

'No.' Tori looked at the slumped figure in the truck's cab, still dangling over the side of the bridge. The carnage of the other vehicles, now even more deformed by the extrication efforts of the fire service, were a reminder of how many people had been seriously injured here, and the enormity of it all really hit home. Tori suddenly felt exhausted. 'I'll stay for a while, too,' she said. 'I'm not sure I'm up to starting a shift in ED just yet.' Taking a deep breath, she exhaled slowly. 'I don't know how you cope with this sort of thing on a daily basis.'

'Big incidents like this are few and far between,' Matt responded. He grinned. 'And you know what we're like in the ambulance service. Being able to do what we're trained for on a scale like this is a highlight of the job.'

That adrenaline buzz might only be a memory now but it was strong enough to make Tori nod slowly.

'It's a very different ball game compared to hospital work, isn't it? You have to be far more self-reliant. Yelling for help isn't necessarily going to get someone who's going to be any more able to deal with the situation.'

'And every challenge is that little bit different. It never gets boring, that's for sure.'

Matt's partner, Joe, was packing away their gear but Matt seemed content to take a break. He leaned against the side of the fire engine beside Tori. 'So, how are you?' he queried. 'It must be nearly six months since I've seen you.'

'That'd be right. You talked me into coming to that

USAR introduction course you ran last year, re-member?'

'Of course I do. You were hopping around on crutches. How's the leg now?'

'Good as new.'

'Did you find the course at all useful?'

'Absolutely.' Tori smiled at Matt. 'That session on triage started flashing like a neon sign in my head as soon as I found I was the first on the scene here.'

'Really?' Matt looked so delighted that Tori found her smile widening.

'Really,' she confirmed. 'It was a great course.'

'You should come and do some more advanced USAR training, then. We could do with some more medically qualified people on the teams.'

'Hmm.' Tori was enjoying the look of genuine interest on Matt's face. His encouraging smile seemed to reach all the way to a pair of equally warm hazel eyes. 'I might just do that.'

For a fraction of a second Matt held her gaze and Tori was reminded of a connection that had been completely buried over the last six months. A base for a friendship that had just been strengthened by what had happened this morning. A friendship she would be more than happy to build on.

Not that she'd want Matt to think she'd changed her mind about anything else, though. Tori broke the eye contact hurriedly.

'How are all the kids?' The reminder of just what had put Matthew Buchanan firmly off any agenda other than friendship was definitely timely.

'Settling in finally, I think. That's why I kind of disappeared for a while. I took a desk job, thinking that the more regular hours would help.'

'And did it?'

Matt shrugged. 'Maybe. Trouble was I missed being on the road too much. In the end I decided that making myself miserable wasn't going to help any of us in the long run. It was rubbing off on the family, no matter how much I tried to hide it.'

Tori found her gaze caught again. He would have tried to hide it, wouldn't he? Anyone who'd been prepared to turn his life upside down and even sacrifice a long-term relationship for the sake of four orphaned nieces and nephews had to be some kind of saint. Or, at the very least, an awfully nice guy.

'So you haven't found anyone to help run the orphanage yet?'

Matt laughed. 'As if! Any sensible woman is going to run screaming into the middle distance at the mention of four kids.'

'True,' Tori grinned. 'You'll just have to find someone who isn't sensible, then.'

'Totally mad, you mean?'

'It might help.' The humour was a thinner veneer than Tori felt comfortable with, however, because she knew better than most the implications of the undercurrents here.

Changing the subject was fortunately effortless enough to be perfectly acceptable. 'Oh, look! They've got the cab of the logging truck onto that crane. It's moving!'

'That's my cue, then.' Matt straightened and watched for a short time as the cab containing the unfortunate driver of the truck swung slowly towards solid ground where it hovered before starting a gentle descent. Matt moved towards the ambulance. 'I'll grab my kit.'

'Can I help?' Tori's exhaustion had mysteriously evaporated. There was, after all, the smallest chance that the truck driver was still alive.

'Joe?' Matt got the attention of his partner. 'Tori's offered to third crew for us for a bit longer. Give her the heavy stuff, eh?'

Joe was grinning as he held out the lifepack. 'If you carry the oxygen cylinder in your other hand, it kind of balances you.'

'Cheers.'

'Just kidding!' Joe put the lifepack on top of the stretcher and then added the oxygen cylinder and suction kit. 'We'll just take the whole bed. Pull out those handles at the end and help me lift it out.'

They had to wait as the cab was very slowly lowered to the ground. Then Matt swung himself up on the step and opened the door. Tori saw him reach to feel for a carotid pulse on the driver's neck.

The shout, seconds later, was astonished.

'Hey...I've got a pulse here. He's *alive*!'

CHAPTER TWO

THIS was a life none of them had expected to save.

For the next fifteen minutes Tori found herself part of a small team working hard to stabilise a critically injured patient who had major chest and head injuries. A body splint and backboard were used, along with a team of firemen, to lift him from the cab of the truck. Matt intubated him to protect his airway and provide adequate oxygenation, and a chest decompression was necessary to deal with the pneumothorax that had caused a lung to collapse and affect his ability to breathe.

It was Tori who helped gain IV access and start fluids running to combat the shocked condition the man was now in. She kept up the monitoring of vital signs, like blood pressure, heart rate and rhythm and the level of respiratory distress, and it was Tori that found the driver's wallet in the back pocket of his jeans.

'His name's Wayne,' she told the others. 'Wayne Judd. He's fifty-three.'

And his driver's licence indicated that he was listed as a potential organ donor. The wallet also included photographs of a woman and children that had to be Wayne's immediate family. Suddenly this patient had a real identity and his willingness to help others if he could no longer be helped himself strengthened the desire Tori felt to see this man survive.

She helped load the stretcher into the ambulance and

switched the tubing from the portable oxygen cylinder over to the wall connection for the main tanks.

Matt had his stethoscope on Mr Judd's chest again. Then he glanced at the oxygen saturation reading on the lifepack.

'He needs IPPV to get those sats up,' he said. 'He's not breathing well enough on his own.'

'I can do that.' Tori moved to the head end of the stretcher. She picked up the bag mask and swiftly changed the connection to the oxygen supply. Swapping the mask on their patient's face, she held the new one securely in place and waited for the chest to rise, indicating an indrawn breath. Squeezing the bag attached to the mask pushed in more air with a high concentration of oxygen that Wayne's lungs, too damaged to inflate deeply enough, were incapable of delivering.

Joe was frowning. It was obvious that close monitoring and possibly further interventions would be necessary *en route* to the hospital. Providing intermittent positive pressure ventilation was all that one person could do.

'We'll have to try and meet some back-up if I'm driving,' he told Matt. 'You'll need some help in the back.'

'I could come,' Tori suggested eagerly. 'My car's still stuck and I should be trying to get into work anyway.'

'Cool.' Matt wasn't going to waste any more time. 'Let's roll.'

Watching pre-hospital emergency care of a critically injured patient on board a rapidly moving ambulance was a totally new experience for Tori, and she was amazed at how Matt made it look so easy. Even trying to get an accurate blood-pressure reading with the interference of engine noise would be a challenge, let alone inserting a second IV line.

Matt's face was serious as he concentrated on his tasks, but he seemed unflappable. Swinging bags of IV fluids smacking the side of his head or keeping his footing during cornering or braking were clearly so much part of his normal working environment he barely missed a beat. He also managed to record a series of vital sign measurements and keep an eye on what Tori was doing.

'Fantastic,' he told her at one point. 'You've got the sats well over 90 per cent now.'

Her glow of pride was out of all proportion to the task, but this was so new for Tori—an extension of the front-line medical management that was so different to her everyday job. The lack of a stable environment, limited resources and total reliance on personal skills made trying to stabilise and transport this patient a challenge that felt almost raw compared to what went on in the emergency department of a large hospital.

What would have been a terrifying responsibility if she had been on her own had become something else entirely. Matt was so confident and obviously skilled that being a part of this drama was exciting. Exhilarating, in fact. It was almost a disappointment to arrive at the Royal's ambulance bay.

Matt had contacted the ED *en route*, relaying all the necessary information about the patient they had on board. They wheeled the stretcher directly into the trauma room, which had been cleared, and a medical team was waiting to take over care of the patient.

'His name is Wayne Judd,' Matt informed the receiving doctor. 'Fifty-three-year-old driver of a logging truck who was trapped in his vehicle for approximately ninety minutes. When we got to him, he was status one, with chest and head injuries. He had a GCS of three, he was tachypnoeic with absent breath sounds on the left side and an oxygen saturation of 83 per cent, BP of 85 over 50 and a heart rate of 130.'

The doctor nodded. 'Let's get him on the bed. I'll take his head.' Staff positioned themselves, leaning over the bed to take a firm grip on the edge of the sheet beneath the patient. Tori lined up with Joe and Matt to lift the sheet on their side of the stretcher.

'On the count of three,' the doctor in charge of the airway instructed. 'One, two…three!'

Maureen, one of the trauma team nurses, moved in to start cutting away the remains of the truck driver's clothing. She caught Tori's gaze.

'You're in trouble,' she whispered. 'Out playing, instead of getting to work on time.'

'I couldn't help it,' Tori protested. 'Pam isn't furious, is she?'

'She hasn't had time to be.' Maureen slipped Wayne's shoes into a paper 'patient property' bag. 'It's been chaos in here.'

Other staff were crowding around the stretcher now and orders were being given for X-rays, CT scans and a neurology consult. Matt and Joe had pushed the stretcher out of the way and were finishing their paperwork in a corner of the room. Maureen took a swift glance at the two ambulance officers as she bundled up the rest of the driver's clothing and put it in the bag. Then she winked at Tori.

'I think I'd stay away and play with those two as well.'

Tori followed her out of the trauma room. It was high time she apologised to the charge nurse, Pam, got herself changed and started work. She certainly didn't want to get caught up in one of Maureen's conversations, which always seemed to be centred on men. Her colleague's attention was not easily diverted, however.

'Who's the new paramedic?' Maureen asked.

'Matt Buchanan. He's not so new. He was around for a little while last year before you started here. He's been off the road for the last six months.'

'You know him?'

Tori nodded. 'I went on a weekend USAR course he ran.'

'Do you know if he's married?'

'Yes.'

'Oh.' Maureen looked crestfallen. 'Why is it that the gorgeous men are all taken by the time I see them?'

Tori had actually meant that she possessed the information but having opened her mouth to correct Maureen's assumption, she promptly closed it again. Matt was probably more than capable of looking after himself, even as the prey of a determined man-hunter like Maureen, but Tori felt absurdly protective. Even more strangely, she took considerable pleasure in extending Maureen's disappointment.

'He's got four kids, too.'

Maureen sighed heavily. 'Well, that's that, then, isn't it?'

'Yep.' Tori saw Pam coming out of a cubicle on the other side of the department and moved to intercept her boss and apologise for her lateness. She passed Matt and Joe coming out of the trauma room with their stretcher, and smiled in response to Matt's grin.

'Catch you later,' she said. 'Don't work too hard.'

'We won't,' Matt assured her. 'Sure you don't want to come and third crew with us for the rest of the shift?'

'I'd love to…' Tori grinned '…but I don't think it would make me any more popular around here.'

They could all see the frown on Pam's face as she watched Tori approach.

'Want me to put in a good word for you?' Matt asked softly.

'Pam's OK. She's just stressed.' Tori waved them through the automatic doors to the ambulance bay. She couldn't help one last glance over her shoulder before moving to appease the charge nurse. Matt and Joe were laughing as they loaded the stretcher, and even from this distance Matt's smile was contagious. As Maureen had said, having four kids ended any possibility of a relationship more than friendship but friends were important, weren't they?

A friend like Matthew Buchanan could quite possibly be the best available. He was a very likable person and now that he was working on this side of town, Tori would be seeing a lot more of him. The thought was enough to buoy her spirits considerably.

'I'm so sorry, Pam. I got caught up in the accident. There really wasn't any way I could have got here earlier.'

The charge nurse nodded then sighed. 'We're short-staffed as it is, and with everyone possible shoved back into the waiting room when we went on code, it's going to be hours before we get back to normal. Get yourself changed and I'll assign your patients. Are you able to stay on a bit later tonight?'

'Sure.' Tori glanced through the doors to the ambulance bay on her way to the locker room and saw the beacons being activated on the ambulance now out on the main road. The sound of the siren kicked in a second later and Tori smiled. There was a bright side to be found here.

The longer she was on duty in the ED, the more chance she had of seeing Matt. And the more she saw of Matt, the more likely it was that they would become friends.

Matthew Buchanan had a lot of responsibilities. He probably had very little time to have fun these days but he seemed like someone who would be very good at it, given the opportunity.

Tori was good at finding opportunities. If they didn't come along by themselves, she was quite capable of engineering them, given an incentive. And the thought of seeing that smile on Matt's face at frequent intervals was an excellent incentive.

But it proved frustratingly difficult to get anything more than brief snatches of conversation with Matt, however hard Tori tried.

The turn-around time for an ambulance crew delivering patients to the emergency department was generally rapid, and Matt and Joe seemed slicker than most. The times they were held up for some reason— by a queue waiting for triage or a bigger than usual clean-up operation before being available for a new job—were invariably the times that Tori was tied up with patient care and could do no more than smile or wave across a busy department.

Happily, Matt seemed as determined as she was to renew their acquaintance. Over the first few days after the incident with the logging truck, both Matt and Joe were keen to get updates on the progress of the accident victims. Tori made sure she kept in touch with what was going on.

Chloe had been the first to go home.

'She got a bright pink cast on her arm,' Tori told Matt the next day. 'She was delighted with it.'

A day later her siblings were allowed to go home with their father.

'Mum's still in ICU but she should go through to a ward later today or tomorrow. She's doing well.'

The male passenger of the car had been transferred to a spinal unit.

'He had a fracture at C6-7,' Tori relayed. 'I'm so pleased I got someone to sit there and hold his head. He's had surgery to stabilise the fracture and he's not showing any neurological deficit.'

The truck driver wasn't doing so well, still in a coma a week after the accident.

'I went up to see him.' Tori shook her head. 'He looks awful! His eyes are completely black and his face is so swollen it's unrecognisable. His wife is in there with him most of the time and she's so grateful for what was done on scene. She tried to thank me but I told her it was you guys who deserved the praise. I'm sure she'd love to say hello to you.'

'We'll try and pop in later maybe.'

'Why don't you go up now?' Joe suggested. 'Control wants us to wait for a patient coming down from plastic Outpatients for a rural transfer. I can go and get her by myself.'

Tori wasn't going to lose this opportunity. 'I'm due for a break,' she informed Matt. 'I'll come with you.'

It was a satisfyingly long trip up to the intensive care unit after they bypassed the lifts and took the stairs.

'This is good,' Tori announced, pushing open the fire

stop door. 'I really needed to get out of the department for a few minutes.'

'It didn't look overly busy.'

'More like boring today. I've had two abdo pains, a ninety-three-year-old with a rectal bleed and a sprained ankle so far. I'm on the trauma team but nothing's come in yet.'

'My apologies,' Matt grinned. 'I'll see if I can arrange a good crash or a nice medical emergency for you.'

'Awful thing to wish for,' Tori admitted. She gave Matt a stern look over her shoulder as she led the way up the stairs. 'I'm blaming you for how tame work seems to be lately.'

'Hey, it's not my fault if people are staying healthy and happy.'

'No, but if I hadn't enjoyed helping at that crash scene so much, I wouldn't have started to notice how ordinary my job is most of the time.'

'So join the ambulance service,' Matt suggested calmly. 'We get our share of boring, though, believe me.'

'Yeah, but when it's not boring, it's *really* not boring.'

'True.'

The easy conversation was interrupted for the short time they spent in the ICU. Mrs Judd was delighted to have the opportunity to thank Matt. She was also a lot happier than the last time Tori had seen her because Wayne was showing signs of regaining consciousness.

'They're keeping him sedated because he still needs the machine to breathe properly, but he opened his eyes this morning and I know he recognised me. He even squeezed my hand.'

'That's great to hear.' Matt smiled.

Colleen Judd had a lot of questions she wanted to ask Matt about the accident and Wayne's rescue, but Tori found her attention wandering. Her nursing career had led very directly to the area she had most wanted to work in and her position in the emergency department represented the goal she had been aiming for.

A career change that might take her in a completely new direction—onto the front line even—had never occurred to her. Until now.

'I might think about what you said,' she told Matt as they made their way back downstairs. 'I could do with a new life.'

'Really? You not happy with the old one?'

Tori could have sworn she read real concern in Matt's eyes and she bit back the denial leaping to her lips.

'It's been a weird few months,' she admitted. 'I'm not enjoying anything right now as much as I used to.'

'What happened to change things?' Matt not only slowed down on the stairs, he paused on the landing. Tori stopped as well.

'It's your fault again,' she said with a grin. 'It was that USAR course that did it.'

Matt raised his eyebrows in both a silent protest and question.

'You remember that cyclone that was happening in the Pacific then?'

Matt nodded but then frowned. 'But USAR didn't get activated for that.'

'They sent a medical relief team, though, and thanks to doing that course, Sarah got called. I couldn't go because my leg wasn't up to it, but she went.'

'Sarah's your sister, yes?'

'Foster-sister really, but we're very close. We were both still living at home and we looked after Mum for ages before she died last year.'

'I'm not quite following how this is my fault yet.' Matt's attention was fully focused on Tori and the sensation was far from unpleasant.

'I went to that course and dragged Sarah along purely for your benefit, you know.'

'Really?'

Tori nodded firmly. 'I'd decided you two were perfect for each other.'

'We were?'

Tori nodded again. 'She loves kids and you're running a private orphanage.'

Matt laughed. 'Hardly. They *are* family.'

'Yeah. And you were just too nice a guy to say no.'

'That's me.'

'Modest as well.' Tori grinned. 'I'm actually quite disappointed you're not going to be my brother-in-law.'

'I haven't had a chance to try,' Matt protested. 'Where's Sarah? Not that I've proposed to anyone for a while, but I'm prepared to give it a shot.'

'I've been trying to tell you,' Tori growled. 'Sas went off to help with that cyclone relief team and she never came back.'

'What?'

'She got kind of involved with someone there. She's living in London now but they're going back to Fiji to get married in a couple of months.'

'I guess she won't want another proposal, then.' Matt shook his head philosophically. 'Story of my life.'

'Well, it's changed my life, too, you know.' Tori sighed. 'I'm living alone for the first time in my life, rattling around in a house that's far too big. Nobody wants to come and live with me because it's too far out of town, and I can't sell up because it's half Sarah's house and, anyway, it's where I grew up so I don't really *want* to sell up.' Tori smiled a little sadly. 'So, here I am with the freedom to be out having a wild old time but instead I'm working all hours and missing having Sas around. My job was what was holding it all together and now—thanks to *you*—I'm starting to feel like it might not be exactly what I want to be doing.'

Matt's pager sounded and he read the message. 'Joe's waiting for me. I'd better head back. Nice long drive out to the country. Hardly an exciting end to the day.'

'Beats being stuck inside, waiting for another sprained ankle or a sore tummy that's going to be around for hours demanding to know why something isn't being done to fix them.'

Matt held the fire stop door open for Tori this time. 'Seeing as it's all my fault that life is less than perfect for you right now, why don't I make amends?'

Despite herself, Tori's heart gave an unusually vigorous thump. There was no disputing Matt's attractiveness, and even being the object of conversational attention was enjoyable. How far would he go to make life a bit more interesting?

'Keep talking,' Tori instructed.

'Come out on the road properly some time. I can arrange for you to be on board as an observer—especially if you are at all interested in changing careers.'

'Who would I go out with?'

Matt grinned. 'I don't think Joe would protest at having you as third crew, and seeing as I've mucked up your life I feel obliged to help you find a bit of excitement again.'

Tori's nod was satisfied. 'Sounds fair to me. I'll talk to my people and get back to you.'

'We're just good friends.'

Tori's airy statement earned her a black look from Maureen, who dropped the magazine she'd been leafing through and stalked out of the emergency department's staffroom.

Erin, the nurse who had brought up the subject of Tori's relationship with Matt, eyed the abandoned seat at the table and gave Tori a meaningful glance.

'Someone's not happy.'

Tori shrugged. 'She's on the hunt for a new boyfriend. She liked the look of Matt.'

'Can't say I blame her.' Erin took another bite of her sandwich. 'So how long have you been seeing him now?'

'I'm not *seeing* him, Erin. When I said we're just good friends, I meant it. I've been out on the road with him a couple of times. I'm seriously thinking of becoming an AO.'

'You're kidding!'

'Nope. I love it. Every job is different and you never know where you're going to be next. We went from this mansion, which actually had a maid to let us in, the other night to an incident at a gang headquarters, where the police had to escort us inside for safety.'

Erin shuddered visibly. 'And what happens when the police aren't there?'

Tori ignored the warning. 'It was a gunshot wound,' she said. 'With a hole in his chest sucking in air. I had to seal it with my hand until we could get an occlusive dressing on it, and then we had to load and go with the armed offenders squad outside dealing with the rival gang.' She sighed happily. 'It was really exciting!'

'I'd rather be in here with a few security guards sitting on the troublemakers,' Erin said firmly. 'In fact, I think I've had about enough of Emergency. I'm thinking of transferring back to Orthopaedics.'

'I love it,' Tori repeated. 'Especially being out with Matt and Joe. They're great fun.'

'Hmm.' Erin's expression was supremely tolerant. 'Just good friends, huh?'

'We're just good friends,' Tori said again later that night when Sarah rang from London. 'He's such a *nice* guy, Sas. Maybe you should reconsider.'

'When I've got Ben? Not in this lifetime, kid!'

Tori suppressed the pang of totally unreasonable envy that Sarah had found 'the real thing'. It wasn't even on her own agenda, was it? Not for years and years, anyway. Good grief, she was only twenty-five and she intended to have as much fun as possible before she settled down to the kind of bliss Sarah was experiencing.

'How's Phoebe?' she asked hurriedly. 'Is she still doing well after the surgery?'

'It's amazing,' Sarah said. 'The tissue expansion created all this perfectly normal skin and they've managed to get rid of all the scar tissue on her face. She's going to look absolutely gorgeous once the swelling's gone down a bit more.'

'That's wonderful.' Tori knew she wasn't sounding as enthusiastic as the news warranted. 'I miss you, Sas.'

'It's not long till the wedding and our plans to emigrate to New Zealand are really taking shape. I've persuaded Ben that living north of Auckland will be perfect. He can commute into the city to work. You'd better start keeping an eye out for properties near you.'

'Maybe you should have this house. It's too big and spooky for just me.'

'Yeah...' Sarah was laughing. 'You could fit Matthew *and* all his kids in there.'

'Don't joke! The thought of taking on someone else's family is a recurring nightmare. You know I had quite enough of foster-children when I was growing up.'

'Hey—I was one of those foster-kids.'

'You were different.' Tori had to swallow a lump in her throat. 'It's so good to talk to you, Sas.'

'Are you all right, Tori? You sound...I don't know...lonely.'

'Who, me? The ''out on the town'' party girl flitting from one romantic adventure to the next? Lonely? Hello-o-o!'

'So what romantic adventures have you not been telling me about, then? The last one I knew about was Robert, and that was a disaster!'

'He *was* the last one,' Tori admitted. 'How sad is that?'

'So get out there and find someone new,' Sarah ordered. 'You obviously like Matt.'

'Matt's out of the question.'

'Why?'

'You know why. He's got four children and no life!'

'You don't have to marry him.'

'He doesn't seem the type to do anything less than serious. And he's too nice for me to want to make his life any more complicated. Besides, I don't want to spend my time off with a bunch of kids.'

'He must escape occasionally.'

'Only to work, from what I can make out.'

'So maybe he needs a chance to have some fun.'

Tori was silent. That thought wasn't totally original, was it?

'And at least he's been upfront about the kids, which is more than Robert was. And he doesn't have a wife tucked away either.'

'Hmm. He's too ugly.'

'I've seen him, remember?'

'Oh…so you have.'

'When are you seeing him again?'

'I'm not *seeing* him. We're—'

'Just good friends,' Sarah interrupted. 'You already said that. So when are you going out on the road with him again?'

'Tomorrow, actually.'

'A night shift?'

'Yeah.'

'Have fun.'

'I'll do my best.' Tori was still smiling well after the phone call had ended. She wouldn't have to try hard. The easy conversation, the humour and the growing friendship made her look forward to his company to the extent that Sarah's suggestion appeared to have some merit.

Later, turning yet again on her pillow as she tried to settle into sleep, Tori decided against offering anything more than friendship, however. There was just something too inherently decent about Matt to contemplate an affair with no strings. Or maybe she just liked him too much.

She had never had a really close male friend without a physical relationship or the desire for one interfering with the friendship on one or both sides. Adding sex to their relationship would be the fastest way to ruin what was promising to be the best friendship Tori had ever had with a man. No matter how attractive Matthew Buchanan was, it wasn't worth the risk.

'And that,' Tori whispered aloud to herself, 'is that. End of story.'

CHAPTER THREE

IT DIDN'T turn out to be much fun after all.

The prospect of another night on the road as an observer with Matt and Joe had been the highlight of Tori's week. The shift started with great promise and the priority-one callout to a car v. pedestrian resulted in an adrenaline-pumping, high-speed obstacle course through rush-hour traffic with Matt's impressive driving skills tested to the limit.

The job was a fizzer, though, and it was almost embarrassing to turn off first the siren and then the beacons, having been informed by the owner of a second-hand furniture shop that the 'victim' had dusted himself off and walked home. Matt and Joe seemed quite philosophical about it, smiling and waving at the group of wide-eyed children who had gathered to watch. Matt blipped the siren in farewell as they pulled away and a small boy could be heard crowing with delight as the noise from the vehicle faded.

The second call, over an hour later, was to a 'sick person' who was apparently unwell enough to also require a priority-one response.

'I'm dying,' he told the crew as he lay on his bed with a damp cloth covering his eyes.

'Don't think so,' Joe said cheerfully. Matt pulled a blood-pressure cuff from the kit and winked at Tori.

'What's been happening?' he queried.

'My head hurts. My eyes hurt. I've got a sore throat.

I ache all over and I feel dizzy when I try and stand up.'

'Anyone else in the family been unwell recently?'

'My wife had the flu last week but she wasn't *this* sick.'

Tori glanced at the woman standing in the doorway of the bedroom with a toddler balanced on one hip and an older child holding her free hand. She probably hadn't had time to be *that* sick.

'Have you seen your GP?'

'No-o-o.' The man groaned rather dramatically. 'I've been too sick to try and get out of bed.'

His wife sighed wearily. 'They don't do house calls any more.'

They listened to their patient's chest, which was clear, took an ECG, which was normal, and pricked his finger to test his blood-sugar levels—also normal. They recorded a normal blood pressure and a slightly elevated temperature. They noted a clean medical history and absence of any prescribed medications.

'You've got the flu, mate,' Joe told him finally. 'You need to rest and keep your fluid intake up. If you take some aspirin or a cold and flu preparation, it'll help the aches and pains. A day or two in bed and you'll be as right as rain.'

'But…you're supposed to take me into hospital, aren't you?'

'We can take you if that's what you really want,' Matt said, 'but you'll be in a very bright, busy, noisy emergency department. You'll be well down any priority list and it could take hours to see a doctor, who will probably send you straight home again with the same advice we've just given you. By then it'll be about 2 a.m. and you will have missed a good few hours' sleep.' Matt's tone became much less forbidding. 'Why don't you try and get some rest at home and see how it goes? You can always call us back if things get worse.'

'Can I?'

'Of course.' Joe was latching the kit. 'That's what we're here for.'

The patient's wife saw them to the door. 'I'm so sorry,' she said. 'I wanted to take him to the after-hours clinic but he really did seem very sick and I couldn't carry him to the car.'

'Man flu,' Tori pronounced as they headed back to station. 'It's a terrible thing.'

'Careful,' Matt warned. 'You're outnumbered right now.'

Tori was unimpressed. 'Let's hope the next one is a female patient,' she said. 'We might actually get a genuine case.'

They had to wait nearly two hours for the next call and the patient was, indeed, a female.

It was also very genuine.

The address was central city, one of a run-down group of old houses that backed onto a commercial and industrial street. Tori eyed the unkempt garden cluttered with rusting car bodies with some misgivings. The house looked equally uninviting. Window-panes were cracked or broken, curtains hung in ragged shreds. The front door stood ajar and revealed a dimly lit hallway strewn with rubbish. A strong smell of cannabis drifted out as they waited for a response to Matt's knock.

'Hello!' Matt moved into the hallway. 'Ambulance here.'

Tori hoisted the weight of the oxygen cylinder to

hold it in her arms. While grateful for the solid presence of Matt and Joe in front of her, knowing she had a potential weapon of her own for self-defence was reassuring.

'Hello!' Matt called more loudly. 'Anyone here?'

A man appeared at a doorway near the end of the hall. Naked to the waist, jeans undone, his body was covered with tattoos. Metal spikes protruded from piercings beneath his bottom lip and added considerably to the belligerent expression on his face. He took the joint of cannabis from where it appeared to be stuck to his lower lip.

'Whaddyawant?'

'Someone called an ambulance to this address.' Matt had stopped and now he moved back in a subtle fashion, which Joe mirrored. Tori found herself surrounded and knew that both these men were poised to protect her if necessary.

'Wasn't me,' the man said.

'She's out the back.' A female voice came from someone still in the room behind the male occupant of the house. 'In the garage.'

Matt turned and touched Tori's shoulder. 'Let's go,' he murmured.

They went out the way they had come in, found a gap between the hulks of wrecked cars and discovered a double garage with its side door hanging open.

Two teenage girls, devotees of Gothic styling, sat on a bare mattress just inside the door. They stared at the newcomers with matching blank faces.

'Hi, there. I'm Matt from the ambulance. This is Joe and Tori. Did you guys call for us?'

'Yeah.' One of the girls pointed to the other side of the garage. 'It's Charlene. She won't wake up.'

Another young girl lay on her side between two mattresses piled with some old blankets and pillows that were losing their stuffing. Matt rolled her over onto her back.

'Charlene, can you hear me? Open your eyes, love.'

There was no response. Even in the dim light provided by the single bare bulb dangling in the centre of the garage Tori could see the blue tinge of cyanosis on the girl's lips.

Joe was uncurling the leads from the life pack to attach electrodes. He cut through a thin sweatshirt to expose what looked like the underdeveloped chest of a child. Having determined that Charlene was not breathing, Matt flipped open the kit and pulled out the bag mask. Tori grabbed the end of the tubing and pushed it onto the oxygen cylinder's connection. She fitted the key to the valve, twisted it open and turned the flow up to fifteen litres a minute—the highest available.

Matt tipped the girl's head back and lifted her chin to open her airway, having checked that there was no obstruction in her mouth. He fitted the mask and inflated the bag twice to deliver two full breaths. Then his fingers went to the side of Charlene's neck.

'No pulse,' he reported grimly.

Joe simply nodded. The display on the screen of the life pack was just settling into a readable rhythm.

'Fine VF,' he announced, equally grim. Tori could understand why. When first in cardiac arrest, a rhythm of ventricular fibrillation was coarse, with the wiggles much further away from a flat base line. There was far more chance of converting a coarse VF into a perfusing rhythm. The longer the 'downtime', the finer the wiggles…and the less hope there was that a life could be saved.

'What's happened here?' Matt directed the question to the girls still sitting near the door. 'How long has she been like this?'

One of the girls shrugged. 'Dunno.'

'Stand clear,' Joe directed. 'Shocking at 200 joules.'

Matt moved backwards so that he wasn't touching the patient. He put the bag mask down and reached for his radio. After a rapid request for back-up to a cardiac arrest, he turned to his kit.

'Could you hold the torch to give me some decent light, please, Tori? I'll intubate in a minute.'

'Sure.' Tori clutched the torch and held it high enough to cast a useful circle of light. She watched in dismay as Joe delivered a second and then a third shock, with no change to the fatal cardiac rhythm displayed on the life pack screen.

Matt unrolled the intubation kit. 'Put the torch down for a sec and hyperventilate her for me, Tori.'

She did as requested, giving the girl as much oxygen as possible before the procedure of securing her airway with the tough, plastic tube. Then she held the torch again, holding her own breath in sympathy with the look of intense focus on Matt's face as he lifted the tongue with the laryngoscope and angled the light on the instrument to visualise the vocal cords.

Tori was ready with the bag mask when Matt had inflated the balloon on the ET tube to help secure its position. He listened for the sound of moving air as Tori squeezed the bag, to ensure it was going into the lungs and not the stomach which would indicate incorrect placement of the tube.

'We're in,' he announced. 'Start CPR, Joe, and I'll get IV access.'

Tori inflated the girl's lungs twice after every fifteen of Joe's chest compressions. They kept it up for a full minute, by which time Matt had an IV cannula inserted and a bag of saline attached. Then Tori sat back to allow Joe to start the next series of three shocks. Matt was drawing adrenaline into a syringe. He looked up as he twisted the top off the second ampoule.

'Somebody needs to tell us what's been going on here,' he told their silent audience. 'It could make a difference to whether we can help Charlene or not.'

His words had an effect. One of the girls burst into tears and the other one put her arms around her.

'Leave her alone,' she shouted at Matt. 'It's not Jamie's fault.'

Tori felt, rather than heard, Matt sigh. 'How old is Charlene?' he asked.

'Fifteen.' The response didn't come from the Goth girls, however. Another girl, dressed in ragged track pants and a T-shirt that did nothing to hide a skeletally thin frame, had entered the garage with an older woman.

'Do you know what she might have taken?'

The new girl received a none-too-gentle elbow from the woman, who succeeded in silencing her. 'They take care of themselves,' the woman snapped at Matt. 'I give them a place to sleep off the streets, that's all. It's none of my business what they get up to.'

Tori squeezed some more oxygen into Charlene's lungs. Her gaze wandered as Joe continued compressions and Matt injected drugs in the hope of restoring a more normal cardiac rhythm.

She could see empty fast-food packages and soft-drink bottles, shoes and clothing in random piles. Empty tins were being used as ashtrays and amongst the piles of empty cigarette packets and other litter she spotted cans of fly spray and air freshener, crumpled rags and a roll of plastic bags. In the dirty blanket folds on the mattress beside Charlene was another aerosol can and a scrunched-up plastic bag.

'I think she's been huffing,' she told Matt.

'Wouldn't be surprised.' Matt shook his head sadly. He had his gaze fixed on the screen. 'Still in VF. I'm going to try an IV bolus of amiodarone.'

The back-up ambulance crew arrived and Tori moved back as her efforts became redundant. She looked at the girls—now both crying—on their mattress and at the folded arms and sullen face of the woman who clearly wanted to avoid any blame for what had happened.

Tori had seen the effects of 'huffing' too many times already in the emergency department of the Royal. Inhalant abuse was the cheapest and most readily available 'high' for young people. Led on by their peer group or unhappy enough to want a reprieve from reality, the users were too young to understand or want to believe how dangerous even a single dose of butane could be. Teenagers were frying their brain cells and sometimes dying for the sake of a thirty to sixty second rush.

And Charlene was one of the unlucky ones. Despite the efforts of both crews for another twenty minutes, there was no return of any spontaneous circulation and once the rhythm had settled into the flat line of asystole, there was no point in shocking the heart again. CPR was finally abandoned after agreement had been sought from all ambulance personnel present, including Tori.

The back-up crew packed up their gear. 'Have the police been informed?'

Matt nodded. 'We'll wait until they get here.'

Quietly, Joe and Tori tidied up. They took the tube from Charlene's mouth and removed the electrodes and defibrillation pads. Matt went to the group of people on the other side of the garage.

'I'm sorry,' he told them. 'We did everything we could to help Charlene but I'm afraid she's died.'

The woman shrugged. 'She was new. I didn't know her, anyway.'

Matt crouched in front of the younger girls. 'I'm sorry,' he said again. His voice was gentle enough to make Tori's eyes prickle with unshed tears. 'Charlene was a friend of yours, wasn't she?'

The girls both nodded. They were clutching each other now and looked too shocked for tears.

'The police are going to have to come,' Matt continued quietly. 'They'll want to talk to you about Charlene.'

The older woman let fly a stream of foul language, then turned abruptly and left the garage. The thin girl who had come in with her stood still for several seconds and then walked towards Tori, who had closed Charlene's eyes and was now gently wiping her face clean with a damp dressing pad. The girl again stood silently, staring at the dead teenager.

'Looks like she's just asleep,' she said finally. She crouched down, staring intently at the pale, still face. 'She's not sad any more. She's lucky, isn't she?'

Tori looked up, alarmed by the note of longing in the girl's tone. What kind of heartbreak led to lives where such an escape could be considered lucky? The girl beside her looked anorexic. Skin was stretched far too tightly over a face probably far older than her years. Jutting collarbones and stick-thin arms around the margins of her T-shirt made her look incredibly vulnerable. Her face was pierced, with three rings through an eyebrow and a stud in her nose. Part of her head was shaved, the rest covered with dreadlocks of varying lengths. Her two front top teeth were broken.

But it wasn't until the girl met her gaze that Tori felt a shock greater than her appearance or even Charlene's death had given her.

'*Monique!*' she whispered.

There was a flicker of acknowledgement on the girl's face.

'It *is* Monique, isn't it? I'm Tori—don't you remember me?'

The girl shrugged. 'I guess. So what?'

Matt had returned to help tidy up. He didn't seem surprised that Tori knew this girl but, then, he probably assumed she had made more than one visit to an emergency department. The bruising and track marks on her bare arms branded her an IV drug user.

The desperation inherent in the lives of those who lived in this squalid garage had suddenly become far more significant to Tori. Unbearable, even. She stood up, moving to reach for the life pack and oxygen cylinder.

'I'll take this lot back out to the truck, shall I?'

A police car had pulled up beside the ambulance.

'She's out the back in the garage,' Tori told them. She led the way back to the scene, answering their initial questions as best she could.

'She's fifteen years old. Her name's Charlene. We haven't been given a surname. There's a group of teenagers who seem to be living rough in there.'

'Anything suspicious about the scene when you arrived?'

Tori shook her head. 'Not really. The girl was lying on the floor beside a mattress. There's plenty of evidence of drug and solvent abuse on the property.'

Matt gave them more information. 'She must have collapsed quite a while before we arrived. She had a fatal cardiac arrhythmia that had deteriorated almost to a standstill. No CPR had been done. We were fighting a losing battle right from the start, really.'

The senior police officer used the beam of his torch to examine the body. 'No sign of external injury, is there?'

'No.'

The torch picked out the can of fly spray in the folds of the blanket. 'Would that be enough on its own to kill her?'

Matt nodded. 'Could well be. The propellant for the spray is butane, which is an asphyxiant. Breathing a gas with absolutely no oxygen in it can cause collapse and death. The toxins can also interfere with the heart's rhythm and cause an arrhythmia that's fatal—like the one Charlene was in when we arrived.'

The police officer looked at Monique. 'Is that what Charlene was doing? Sniffing?'

Monique shrugged a painfully bony shoulder. 'We do it all the time. Doesn't kill you.'

'Sometimes it does,' Matt told her firmly. 'It might happen the first time you try it. Or it might just be that you have a bit more than you did last time and that'll be enough to kill you this time.'

Tori could see the flash of fear in Monique's eyes but it was quickly shuttered. 'So?' The bravado was a practised shield. 'Who gives a stuff, anyway?'

It was a relief to leave the police in charge of the scene, but the job couldn't be left behind as far as Tori was concerned. Every detail stayed with her over the next two jobs the crew were assigned to. Even the distress of a woman who feared she was having a miscarriage couldn't obliterate the misery she had found in that garage.

Joe took advantage of the quiet spell in the early hours of the morning to lie down on one of the couches in the staff commonroom on station. Matt made two cups of coffee and sat down at the table beside Tori.

'You're very quiet,' he observed. 'Want to talk to Uncle Matt?'

Tori tried to smile. 'I'm OK.'

'It wasn't a nice job.' They both knew he wasn't referring to the threatened miscarriage. 'I hope you haven't been put off ambulance work.'

'It's nothing I haven't seen before,' she admitted. 'It's just that it's so different, seeing it happen away from the hospital. It makes it…I don't know, more real somehow. They aren't brought in to us. We go there— into their lives. Into their homes.'

'If you could call that a home.'

'I think that's what really got to me. Apart from feeling frustrated that we were too late to help Charlene, I can't help feeling guilty that we couldn't do something to help those other girls.'

'The police will bring the social services in. Those girls will be returned to their families, I would think. They must be under age.'

'But that probably won't help,' Tori said miserably. 'There was a reason they ran away and ended up on the streets in the first place, wasn't there?'

'It's not your fault, Tori,' Matt said gently. 'Don't be so hard on yourself. We can only do the best we can. No matter how much we'd like to, we can't get out there and save the world.'

'But I didn't even try,' Tori whispered. To her dismay, a tear rolled down her face. And then another.

'Hey...' Matt's chair scraped on the linoleum as he moved closer. His arm was an instantly comforting weight on her shoulders. 'What's all this about, Tori? What's upset you so much?'

'Monique.'

'The skinny girl?'

'She didn't used to be skinny. She was really pretty eight years ago.'

'How on earth did you know her eight years ago?'

Tori scrubbed at her tears. 'She came to live with us,' she told Matt. 'My mother wanted to save the world. Or at least as many unhappy kids as she could. She started taking in foster-children when I was two, after my dad died.'

Matt gave her shoulder an encouraging squeeze and then dropped his arm. 'Drink your coffee,' he instructed Tori, 'and tell me all about it.'

'Monique was probably the least successful,' Tori responded. 'She only lived with us for about three months. She stole stuff, she swore at everybody, she ran away from school. She ran away from home every few days.'

Tori held on to her mug but didn't raise it to her lips. 'I hated her,' she confessed. 'She called my mum a stupid bitch. She scratched Sarah's face badly. She stole all my make-up and just helped herself to my clothes. She even tried to seduce my boyfriend, and she was only twelve, for God's sake!' Tori shook her head. 'It wasn't until she tried to set fire to the house that Mum admitted defeat and let Social Services take her away. Monique was really upset about it.'

Matt didn't break the short silence that fell so Tori kept talking.

'Maybe she knew how she'd end up if somebody didn't keep trying. I didn't know—I didn't even want to think about it, I guess. I just wanted her out of our lives.' Looking up, Tori found the understanding in Matt's hazel eyes almost painfully intimate.

'How old were you?'

'Sixteen. Almost seventeen.'

'You were still a child. You can't beat yourself up for being a perfectly normal teenager. The vast majority of adults would have felt the same way, come to that.' Matt smiled. 'Your mum must be one special lady.'

'She was. She died last year.' Tori had to look away from Matt so that she didn't start crying again. 'I couldn't do it. Even though I love Sarah just as much as I would if she were my birth sister, I couldn't do what Mum did. If I have kids, they're going to be my own. A *real* family. Not something cobbled together with bits that don't fit, because when you try to force them to fit you end up breaking what's already there.'

Tori bit her lip as she heard her own words and realised the implication. 'Oh, I'm sorry, Matt. I wasn't thinking. I didn't mean—'

'It's OK,' Matt interrupted. 'I understand.'

He did, too. She could see that in his eyes, but Tori still felt like she had given him a knock he didn't need.

Or deserve. She could have hurt him, and that was something she wasn't going to allow.

'Mum *was* a very special person. Sarah's got that gift of accepting and loving people as well. So have you, Matt. I really admire what you've done for your nieces and nephews. You want to know something else?'

'What?'

'You're the *nicest* person I've ever met.'

Her smile was quite genuine this time and Tori hoped her gaze conveyed her gratitude for his ability to listen and accept her position. For a few seconds Matt held her gaze and smiled back, and the warmth of the connection Tori felt with this man was so strong it could only be love.

Not the in love sort of love. It went deeper than that in a different direction. It was more like the kind of love she'd had for her mother and still had for Sarah. A bond of something a lot more than simply friendship.

Matt's smile faded first. He shook his head.

'I'm not some kind of saint,' he told her. 'I did what I had to do, that's all. And I know exactly where you're coming from, Tori. I have my share of moments when I really resent the whole situation. Occasionally, I'd just like to wave a wand and make them all go *poof*. I'd like,' he said softly, 'to have my own life back again.'

Their mugs of coffee had gone cold but neither of them noticed. They sat at the table in a puddle of light that enclosed them in a space all their own. Joe was snoring quietly on the couch and Matt's voice was too low to disturb his partner.

'And then,' Matt continued, 'I get a job like that one tonight and I know that, no matter how hard it is sometimes, I did the right thing. If I hadn't taken the kids they could well have ended up in foster-homes and they would have been separated. Hayley's fifteen. Same age as Charlene. She's your typical bolshy teenager, only worse. She was the most badly affected by the deaths of her parents. She covers it up by being moody and unpleasant, but I know that on some level she blames herself for the accident and she feels she should be able to care for her brothers and sisters. And, of course, she can't.'

'Why would she blame herself?'

'There'd been an argument. Hayley had been invited to a party and she didn't want to do the babysitting she'd agreed to. Jane and Graeme ended up being late leaving and could well have been speeding. The weather was the usual foul January stuff in London and there was a freezing fog on patches of the A1 that night. A lethal combination, as it turned out.'

'Jane was your sister, yes?'

Matt nodded. 'She was nearly sixteen years older than me.' He grinned. 'I was a bit of an afterthought. I'm thirty-two but my parents are in their early seventies now. They're still fit and healthy and they would have taken the kids on themselves, but it would be too much for them and, besides, I was far more a part of their world. The only adult they had left, in fact.'

'How long had you lived in England?'

'Just over eleven years. I took off after I finished a science degree at uni and I lived with Jane and Graeme for a while. Hayley was only three then and her brother Charles was a baby. The twins came along five years later so I knew them right from day one.'

'You were still living with them?'

'Oh, no. I'd sorted myself out by then and had a

career and my own home. Even a fiancée. Sandra, her name was. I still spent a lot of time with Jane and Graeme and the kids, though. They were such a happy family, you know? It was something I really wanted for myself. I thought Sandra did, too. My future seemed really well mapped out.'

Tori felt a flash of contempt for the woman who Matt had once told her had given him the ultimatum of choosing between her and his orphaned relatives. Then she realised, with more than a little shame, that she would have been just as likely to refuse such involvement with someone else's children. Amazing that Matt was even prepared to be friends with her really, but, then, he'd known how she felt right from the start, hadn't he? He might understand why after their conversation tonight but he'd been prepared to accept her anyway. He was, without doubt, rather an extraordinary person.

'You'll find someone else, Matt. Someone who really appreciates how special you are.'

As she, herself, did?

'Maybe.' Matt's snort was dubious, however. 'When the kids have left home and I'm old and grey.'

'But don't your parents help out? Surely you could get out on a date now and then.'

'Of course I could. In fact, I got asked out only last week by a nurse in your department. That one with the black hair and a bit too much make-up?'

'Maureen.' The word came out in almost a growl and Tori tried to push down the flash of jealousy that was even more unreasonable than her contempt for Sandra had been. Then she brightened. 'You didn't accept, then?'

'Hardly.' The huff of expelled air was dismissive.

'I'm not after sex for its own sake. It might sound corny, but I'm probably after the same thing you want, Tori. To find a soul-mate. To have a family of my own.'

They both fell silent now. It was too obvious how hard it was going to be for Matt to achieve a perfectly natural dream. Tori had far more chance of success but, instead of making her feel relieved, the knowledge created a wash of something more like guilt.

'You need to get out more,' she decided aloud. 'That's the only way to meet people. *I* need to get out more as well. I've been in a decline since Mum died and Sarah left. We should go out together and paint the town red one night.'

Matt looked unconvinced. 'I've been out of circulation for so long, a night's clubbing would probably kill me.'

The reminder of the tragedy the night had provided was unavoidable. Tori's suggestion seemed suddenly shallow. Inappropriate.

'Maybe a holiday is what you really need,' she said. 'A few days' break. Some time just for yourself.'

'Taking a holiday alone doesn't have much appeal either.'

'Go with a friend, then.'

'I haven't had the chance to get to know too many people on this side of the world yet. Except for all the mothers who pick their kids up from school at the same time I do.'

'You'd better be careful there,' Tori warned. 'You could end up with eight kids instead of four!'

'Perish the thought.' But Matt was smiling again. 'I could ask Joe, but that might raise a few eyebrows

around here.' He looked thoughtful. 'I could ask
Maureen, I suppose, if I got really desperate.'

Tori shook her head emphatically. 'You get too
many things expected from you at home, don't you?
You need to go away with no strings attached.'

'You could be right. Maybe I do need to be a bit
more selfish occasionally. Just for a few days here and
there. Where do you think would be a good place to
go?'

'I don't need to think,' Tori told him happily. 'I
know.'

The idea had come in a flash of pure brilliance. She
leaned forward, her tone deliberately seductive. 'What
about a private, tropical island? Sunshine and sand and
the bluest, warmest ocean imaginable to swim in? I'll
even throw in a party...with champagne!'

Matt laughed. 'Oh, babe. Bring it on!'

'I'm serious,' Tori said sternly. 'I'm going to Sarah's
wedding in three weeks' time and they've sent me two
tickets so I can bring a partner. Ben *owns* this island
and there's heaps of room for visitors.'

'Did Sarah know you were trying to set me up with
her when you both came to that USAR course?'

'That doesn't matter.' Tori grinned wickedly. 'I tried
to hit on Ben before he and Sarah got it together so it
would kind of even things out.'

'No way! I'm not getting into some weird sibling
rivalry thing here.'

'Come on, Matt. It would be *fun*! It's just what you
need. What we both need. A weekend away with a
mate. No strings. We could just enjoy ourselves.'

Her efforts hadn't quite succeeded, she could tell.
Her face stilled and her voice softened. 'It's going to
be a bit lonely for me,' she confessed, 'watching my

sister getting married. I could really do with a friend to hold my hand.'

Matt wasn't smiling any more either. He stared at Tori and they both jumped as his pager sounded.

'Chest pain,' he reported, reading the message. Joe stirred on the couch, groaning.

Matt pushed his chair back and stood up. 'It's a priority one,' he told Tori. 'Are you coming?'

She grinned. 'I was just about to ask you the same question about Sarah's wedding. How 'bout we both say yes?'

'I'll have to think about it.'

'Just say yes,' Joe mumbled through a yawn. 'You can think too much, you know, mate. Especially at this time of night.'

'You could be right.' Matt followed Joe towards the waiting ambulance, turning to grin at Tori over his shoulder. 'I can't promise I'll be able to come,' he told her. 'But I'll certainly see what I can do.'

CHAPTER FOUR

'OF COURSE you should go, darling.'

'Hmm. Maybe.'

Linda Buchanan looked up as she started moulding another spoonful of cookie dough.

'You really mustn't let these children take over every minute of your life. It's not good for any of you.'

She put the ball on the oven tray and smiled at her son, but there was concern etched into the line that appeared between her eyebrows.

'You look tired, Matt. Are you sure you're coping?'

'It's been a tough week, Mum, that's all. I'm fine.' Matt reached out and helped himself to a ball of cookie dough.

Linda clicked her tongue and made a half-hearted move to smack his hand, but she was laughing now. 'And I thought I was keeping the trouble-makers *out* of my kitchen!'

They both looked out the window over the sink to where Bob Buchanan was climbing off a stepladder, having fixed a basketball hoop to the side of the garage. Seven-year-old twins Bonnie and Jack were bouncing up and down, both clutching shiny new orange balls. Jack clearly couldn't wait any longer and his aim wasn't bad for a first effort, but the ball missed the hoop and hit his grandfather on the side of his head.

The ladder wobbled precariously. Linda caught her breath in dismay and the twins stood open-mouthed with horror, but Bob made it safely to the ground and appeared to be shaking his head and laughing as he folded the ladder and propped it up on the fence.

'They're a handful,' Linda murmured fondly. 'I don't know where they get their energy from.'

'I think they got the share that should have gone to Hayley and Charles. I can't get Hayley out of bed before 11 a.m. if it isn't a school day, and then she'd rather sit around watching TV or listening to music.'

Linda followed Matt's gaze as he turned to look through the serving hatch on the other side of the kitchen. Hayley was lying on the couch in the living room, earphones over her long, mousy hair, and she was leafing through the pages of a magazine. Twelve-year-old Charles was sprawled on the floor, trying to fit the latest component of the plastic skeleton that came with the 'Human Body' books into place. Matt glanced at Hayley again and sighed.

Another row of balls had appeared on the oven tray. 'You should let me do more to help, Matt. I don't like the way you don't sleep properly after your night shifts.'

'I sleep once I get the kids to school.'

'Not yesterday.'

'I'm hoping that won't happen again. I've had a good talk to Hayley. I think having a parent called to remove her from the school was embarrassing enough to have an effect.'

'You should have called me, love. I would have gone to get her.'

'You do enough, already, Mum. You and Dad. I'd never manage without you.'

It was Linda's turn to sigh. 'You shouldn't have to manage. Not at your age. Not by yourself.'

'It's probably just as well I didn't marry young and

have my own family. There's not many marriages that could have taken the strain of four extra kids landing on the doorstep.'

'You could always hire a nanny. The trust fund for the children must be looking pretty good now that Jane and Graeme's house has been sold.'

'Money isn't the issue.' Matt waited until his mother's attention was focused on scraping the mixing bowl and stole another raw cookie. 'The kids have had the bottom fall out of their world. I'm providing the only real continuity and I don't want them to lose any of that before the dust has really settled. That's why I'm not sure about going away. I have a suspicion that mentioning it was enough to cause Hayley's bad behaviour at school yesterday.'

'I can't believe she swore at her teacher!' Linda shook her head sadly. 'It's only for a weekend. It'll do you good. Your dad and I aren't going to crack under the strain, you know. And the children seem to enjoy being here.'

Shrieks of glee could be heard from beneath the basketball hoop now, but the drain on energy levels seemed to be centred on Bob who was having to make frequent trips into the neighbour's front yard to retrieve large orange balls. Linda paused to watch them again before opening a drawer.

'We'd hardly know these children if they were still living in London. A visit once a year or so and that would have been it. In some ways, all this has been a real blessing for us.' Picking up a fork, she began flattening the biscuits. 'Now, tell me again. Who's getting married?'

'Sarah. She's a nurse I met last year when she came to a USAR course they talked me into running. It's her sister I know better, though. Tori was one of the first people I met when I started work in Auckland. She's a nurse in Emergency but she's been out on the road a few times with me recently. I think I've almost persuaded her to join the ambulance service.'

'Tori's an unusual name.'

'It's short for Victoria.' Matt found himself smiling. 'Which wouldn't suit her at all. There's nothing strait-laced about Tori. She's great fun.'

'Oh?' Linda's quick glance made Matt shake his head.

'We're just good friends, Mum. There's no chance of anything more than that.'

'Oh.'

The disappointment in his mother's tone struck a familiar chord and Matt pretended to watch the twins' goal-shooting efforts to avoid an explanation. His mother was already concerned about the effect his instant family was having on his life, and he knew that she was quite capable of worrying to the point of making herself unwell. He couldn't let her know that he had, more than once, been far more disappointed than she was.

If Linda was waiting to hear more, she gave no sign of it. The tray of biscuits slid into the oven and she turned her attention to preparing vegetables for dinner. Matt picked up a potato peeler.

'Why don't I do that? You should go and put your feet up.'

'I'll need to get those biscuits out of the oven in a few minutes.'

'I can do that.'

'The meat needs to go in the oven when the biscuits come out.'

'I can do that, too. Go on, shoo!' Matt's smile took any bossiness out of his tone. 'Charles is dying to tell you about his skeleton and you never know—Hayley might even feel like talking.'

The mechanical task of peeling vegetables did nothing to dispel the echoes of regret left from that single syllable his mother had uttered. And that flash of interest in her glance had been just as familiar. Matt had experienced it, with bells on, the first time he had laid eyes on Victoria Preston—nearly a year ago now, when she had been in animated conversation with colleagues in the staffroom at the Royal's emergency department.

Even with her leg in a walking brace and a pair of crutches propped up in a corner of the room, Tori had exuded energy and sheer *joie de vivre*. Blonde curls bounced when she laughed, and clear blue eyes shone with mirth and mischief.

Charles sounded like he was glowing with a similar enthusiasm as he showed his grandmother his latest junior anatomy publication.

'There's heaps of different sorts of joints, Nanna. Ball and socket, like in your hip, and a hinge, like in your elbow. And you've got a pivot joint in your neck so your head can go round.'

'Yeah...' His older sister's tone suggested resentment at Linda's focus of attention. '*Your* head can go right round. Three hundred and sixty degrees—like in *The Exorcist*.'

'That's just special effects,' Charles said loftily. 'Nobody's head can go *right* round.'

'Of course not,' Linda agreed.

'Duh!' Hayley shook her head in disgust and dropped her magazine. The look she threw in Matt's direction let him know that he was failing to make life even remotely interesting and that, in fact, he was probably contributing to it being less than satisfactory.

Matt ignored the look and smiled at his niece. 'I can find a job for you if you're bored, Hayley.'

'Nah. I'm good.' Hayley fished her cellphone from the pocket of very low-slung jeans and began texting furiously.

Matt hid a smile as he picked up another potato. At least Hayley had made some friends now. She'd had difficulty hiding how thrilled she had been with the gift of a cellphone last Christmas. While she covered up her lack of self-esteem and rather painful shyness with a 'couldn't give a damn' bravado, Matt knew perfectly well how desperate she had been for friendship with her peers, and being able to stay in virtually constant communication was a key to belonging these days.

His thoughts drifted almost automatically back to Tori and that first meeting. Matt doubted she had ever had any issues with shyness as a teenager, or, if she had, they had been long since conquered. Maybe it had been that total lack of reticence on her part that had drawn him out so quickly when they had found themselves alone in the staffroom only minutes after their introduction.

Or was it more that easy familiarity that made him feel like he'd known Tori for ever? That he could talk to her about anything at all? He had, hadn't he? Right from the start. He'd kept it light, but making jokes didn't cover the reality that he'd practically cried on her shoulder about the difficulty of starting a new life with the unexpected responsibility of four children, and that his fiancée had dumped him when he had refused to give them up.

She had been very sympathetic, but the fact that her sympathies had been with Sandra had been a little harder for Matt to laugh about. When she had widened those blue eyes and shaken her curls, declaring that four unexpected children would be *her* worst nightmare as well, the shaft of disappointment had speared something deep inside Matt. The fact that his adopted family made it impossible to follow up the extraordinary attraction this woman held for him had also allowed the first seeds of resentment to bloom.

He'd stamped on them, though. He'd made his choice and it had been the right one. The presence of Tori and her sister at that USAR course may have fed the attraction but, in the position of instructor, Matt had found it easy enough to maintain his distance. Tori had made it quite clear she wasn't interested and when he'd given in to the strong impulse to be near her and had joined her in the first coffee-break, she had all but pushed him into the arms of her sister and left them to 'get to know each other'. Sarah had been perfectly lovely but there had been no spark there—on either side.

And he couldn't afford sparks at this point in his life. Or, rather, he couldn't allow sparks to kindle anything. As he'd said to Linda, these children needed stability. A time for the dust to settle and for them to come to terms with the tragedy that had marred their childhoods. Hayley was the most vulnerable right now. The twins would accept anyone who came into their lives offering love. Charles would keep his distance and weigh things up carefully, but his loyalty would be won by the right person. Hayley was a completely different kettle of fish.

A terrifying one.

Matt's hands stilled for a moment as he watched his father come into the house. Hayley pulled away from his touch but her gaze clung jealously to her grandfather as he ruffled her brother's hair and crouched to admire the skeleton.

Matt could feel the emotional tightrope Hayley walked. She pushed people away in an attempt to find independence and self-reliance, but she craved the safety of childhood and the love that was freely offered around her. His heart ached for his niece and Matt vowed not to let her attitude annoy or baffle him so much. She might be the hardest of the children to love, but she needed him more than the others right now. The last thing Matt could afford to do would be to dilute his available attention by including a lover in his life.

And that thought spiralled neatly back to Tori and almost instantly from Tori to the job they had recently shared. To that dimly lit garage and the ongoing tragedy of the lives of those teenagers. How much balance would have to be lost before Hayley fell off that tightrope and found herself on a path similar to Charlene's? Matt wasn't going to let that happen. No way!

'Something's burning, Matt!' Linda was scrambling to her feet. 'Did you take those biscuits out of the oven?'

'Oh…*no*!' Matt dropped the peeler and grabbed an oven mitt, but it was too late. The chocolate chip cookies were blackened around the edges and starting to smoke.

Removing them from the oven set off the smoke alarm in the kitchen. Linda opened windows and Bob flapped a teatowel to try and silence the strident siren of the alarm. Charles came to peer through the serving hatch, his mouth open at the spectacle, and Hayley scooped her magazine off the floor and prised herself off the sofa. A door slammed after her.

'I'm so sorry, Mum.'

'It doesn't matter, darling.'

'Uncle Matt! Uncle *Matt*!'

The cry came loudly through the opened window and it was followed by a howl of pain. Matt dropped the mitt on top of the still smoking biscuits and stepped to the window. It was Bonnie yelling for him. Jack lay in a small crumpled heap beside an overturned stepladder.

Matt was outside in seconds with Charles and Linda on his heels.

'What happened?'

'Jack got the ladder so he could get the ball through the hoop easier, but he fell off!'

'Jack?' Matt crouched beside the boy. 'What hurts, buddy?'

'My arm! *Ow!*'

Bob, the teatowel still clutched in his hand, arrived and Hayley turned up in his wake to add to the audience.

'It's OK, mate.' Matt held the child as he struggled to sit up. 'Did you hit your head?'

'No-o!'

'Let me just have a feel of your neck. Does this hurt?'

'No. Ow-w! My arm!'

They could all see that it was broken. A Colles' fracture of the wrist had Jack's left hand angled down like the end of a dinner fork. Having established that no other injuries had been suffered, Matt took charge of the treatment.

'Hayley, can I borrow your magazine?'

'What for?'

'I'll show you. Dad, can I have that teatowel? And Charles, can you go to the first aid kit in the car and find me a bandage, please?'

They all watched as Matt rolled the teatowel into a sausage that fitted under Jack's hand and supported the distorted shape of his forearm. The magazine rolled around the arm from elbow to fingertips and made a perfect, firm splint once bandaged into place. Matt felt for a pulse and pressed one of Jack's nails to check capillary refill, then he smiled at his nephew.

'Is that feeling a bit better?'

'It still hurts.'

'I know, buddy. We'll have to take you into hospital now so it can be fixed up properly.'

Bonnie burst into tears but Charles tugged at Matt's elbow. 'Can I come, Uncle Matt? Please?'

'Sure.' Matt noticed how anxious Charles was looking. 'What do you reckon, mate?' he asked softly. 'Has Jack broken his radius or his ulna?'

'Maybe both.' Charles chewed his lip to help him think. 'Is he going to be all right?'

'He'll be fine.' Matt scooped Jack up into his arms. Very pale, the child was uncharacteristically quiet and still.

Bonnie clung to her grandmother, sobbing. 'Don't take him away, Uncle Matt. *Don't!*'

Matt caught his mother's gaze and they both nodded. Bonnie needed to come as well. To leave her wondering if her twin would return from a hospital after having an accident would be too cruel.

'I'll turn the oven off,' Bob decided. 'I think we'd better all come for the ride.'

'What for?' Hayley was glaring at Jack. 'It's only a broken arm.'

'We're family,' Matt reminded her gently. 'You'd want us to look after you if you got hurt, wouldn't you?'

'I'm not stupid enough to fall off a ladder,' Hayley mumbled, but she climbed into the back of Matt's roomy car with no further objections. 'I suppose I'll have to come if I want my magazine back.'

'Wouldn't Auckland Central be closer?' Linda was looking over her shoulder as Matt eased into the lane that would take them over the harbour bridge.

'Yes, but I've got friends at the Royal,' Matt told her. 'Having five extra family members accompanying a patient might make us a bit unpopular anywhere else.' He indicated another lane change. 'Besides, it's Saturday. The traffic won't be too bad.'

It had been a perfectly valid desire to keep the family together as much as possible that had prompted Matt's decision to head for the Royal. He wasn't going to admit to anyone, including himself, the even stronger desire to see Tori. She probably wasn't even on duty, but if she was, her smile could provide a ray of light at the end of the tunnel he was currently negotiating.

Jack's broken arm was the culmination of a hideous week. Work had been tough but the hassles of his home life had been a lot tougher. Chores had been neglected and homework had been lost. Charles had had toothache, which had resulted in him having to miss his classical guitar lesson. As passionate about his music as he was about anatomy, the upset hadn't been helped by a long wait and then painful treatment at a dentist's rooms. The wet, cold weather had given the twins cabin fever, which had led to incessant and surprisingly contagious squabbling. The trouble Hayley had got herself into at school and the lack of sleep for Matt after a hard night shift had seemingly been the worst of it.

Until now. Matt glanced over his shoulder to where Linda was cradling Jack as best she could, with the safety belts they both wore. The small boy looked as miserable as Matt had ever seen him. And Bonnie looked terrified. Pretty much the way they had both looked on the day of their parents' funerals.

Boy, did he need a friend right now. Not just any friend. He wanted to tell Tori all about his nightmare week and be able to make a joke about it and hear her laugh, knowing that there was genuine sympathy beneath the humour. He couldn't let on to his parents how hard this all was. He was thirty-two years old, for heaven's sake, he didn't need to run to his parents for comfort. But if he didn't laugh about it, he might cry. And that wouldn't help any of them, would it?

It wasn't until he saw who was standing beside the triage nurse as he led the whole Buchanan tribe into the Royal's emergency department that Matt realised just how much he had been longing for Tori's company. He had to swallow a lump in his throat, and Tori wasn't smiling either. Her eyes widened dramatically and her jaw dropped.

'Matt! What on earth's happened?'

'Jack, here, has hurt his arm. He fell off a ladder.'

'Oh…no!' Tori reached out and brushed a blond curl back from Jack's forehead as he lay in Matt's arms. 'Does it hurt, sweetheart?'

'Ye—e—es.'

'You're being very brave, then.' Tori smiled at Jack, her fingers still resting lightly on his hair.

'This is Tori, Jack.' Matt ignored the sudden attention of Linda, who was standing to one side, holding Bonnie's hand. 'She's a friend of mine. She might be able to look after you, if we're lucky.'

'Uncle Matt's looking after me,' Jack told Tori.

'Of course he is.' Tori nodded. 'But I can help, can't I?' Matt considered her smile more than enough to win someone over. Tori turned to the triage nurse. 'Erin, I'll take this lot, OK?' Her gaze shifted direction again swiftly. 'You must be Mrs Buchanan. Jack's grandma.'

'Nanna.' Linda certainly seemed to have been won over by the welcoming smile. 'I'm Linda.'

'It's lovely that you could all come in with Jack. Could I get you or Mr Buchanan to talk to the clerk over here? Once we've got the paperwork started, we can get things moving quickly.'

Bob went to answer questions and Hayley hung back, clutching her phone and staring around the department as though she'd landed on an alien planet.

'We'll get you straight through to Orthopaedics,' Tori told Matt. 'We just need to book Jack in and get a doctor to eyeball him.' Her attention was on the whiteboard behind the triage desk now. 'Erin, is it OK if I put us in a resus area for now? There's more room for the family that way.'

'Sure. You might need to vacate in a hurry if we get an emergency in, though.'

Tori nodded. 'I'll find some chairs.' Her glance towards Hayley was casual but her tone firm. 'Can you turn your cellphone off, please, love? They can interfere with some of the equipment in here.'

'But—'

'I'll show you where you're allowed to use it later.' Tori was leading the group towards Resus 3, seemingly unaware of the black look being directed at her. 'But turn it off for the moment, thanks.'

Several pillows were propped up against the sloping end of the bed in Resus 3. Matt gently deposited Jack who squeaked in discomfort as his uncle eased a pillow under the splinted arm.

'Does he need IV pain relief?' Tori queried.

'He's been reasonably comfortable since I put the splint on.'

'That's my magazine.' Hayley had moved to the far corner of the resus area and was still glaring at Tori.

Tori ignored her. 'I'll set up some Entonox.'

Charles had his head tipped back, light glinting off his spectacles as he stared at the room's fitting. 'What's that for?'

'Oxygen,' Matt told him. 'And that's suction.'

'What's suction?'

'Kind of a human vacuum cleaner. You use it to get things like spit out of someone's mouth if they can't breathe properly.'

'Eeew!' Hayley said loudly. 'That is so gross!'

'And this is for blood pressure.' Tori moved to stand closer to the bed. 'Have you ever had your blood pressure taken, Jack?'

'No-o-o.'

Tori smiled reassuringly at the fearful tone. 'It doesn't hurt, sweetie. It just squeezes your arm a bit. Shall we get Charles to try it first?'

Charles blinked but then a smile tugged at the corner of his mouth. 'Cool.' He pushed up the sleeve of his sweatshirt. 'Do I get to have an X-ray, too?'

Matt was silent as he stood close to Jack while Tori took baseline vital signs. Charles was put in charge of taking Jack's pulse and he took the responsibility very seriously, counting for a full minute. Linda sat on a chair with Bonnie on her lap, and Matt could see that they were both watching Tori with fascination. When she took a moment to grab a glove, blow it up and knot the end to make a balloon for Bonnie, even Hayley was watching. Tori used a felt-tip pen to draw rooster markings on the glove, glancing up to wink at Hayley.

'I'd offer you one, but I'm sure you'd rather just have your magazine back.'

Matt made the mistake of catching his mother's gaze at one point. She might as well have had a balloon over her head with the words 'Why not? She's so good with the kids…see?'

He shook his head imperceptibly. The disappointment was still fresh for Linda, but the length of time that Matt had spent away from the road at that desk job had been enough for it to have morphed into regret for him. And even that had faded. It was the way things were, and that was that. A case of accepting what couldn't be changed.

Meeting Tori again hadn't sparked anything more than an appreciation of her company. Spending time with her on the road had deepened that to a genuine affection that made friendship with her a very desirable commodity, and that friendship had developed a whole new level after the night young Charlene had died.

They understood each other. The odd glance that came his way while Tori busied herself looking after Jack had been more than enough to let Matt know that she knew exactly how close to the end of his tether he was in his role as a parent. When he got the chance, he'd be able to tell her just how awful the whole week had been. He could even admit his moments of utter despair at the task he'd taken on, and she would not only understand but she wouldn't think any the less of him for it.

And he understood exactly why she would never share any more of her life with someone else's children. It wasn't that she didn't care. She'd been there and done that and had the scars to prove it. If she wanted to protect herself from now on, it was more than understandable. It was commendable. Matt approved, in fact. He'd like to protect Tori himself, and the way he could do that was to make sure he never revisited thoughts of anything more than friendship.

Could he keep himself in that safe place if he went away with her for a weekend? Was that, rather than its effect on the children, what was giving him second thoughts?

Disturbingly, Linda seemed to guess what Matt was thinking about. When they were about to wheel Jack through for his X-ray, she smiled at Tori.

'It's your sister that's getting married next weekend, isn't it?'

Tori nodded. 'I can't wait. A couple of days of sunshine and sea will be a real treat.'

'Matt's looking forward to it as well.'

Tori's pleasure was more than evident in the smile she directed at Matt. 'Have you decided, then? You're going to come with me?'

Matt waited until they had left the rest of the family behind them. 'I'd like to,' he admitted. 'I could really use a break right now.'

'But?'

Matt grimaced. 'Hayley's being difficult.'

Tori grinned. 'She's a teenager. It's in her job description. She's not going to respect you if you let her walk all over you, Matt. Kids need boundaries to push to declare independence. If they can't find the boundaries, they'll just keep pushing until they do. Let Hayley win this one and she'll be twice as difficult the next time you want to do something for yourself. It's only for a couple of days.'

It was a more considered version of what his mother had said earlier, wasn't it? Maybe Matt's approach wasn't that good for any of them, but that was hardly surprising, was it? He'd been thrown into parenthood at the deep end. The thought of Hayley being twice as difficult next time round was scary, but the teenager wasn't Matt's only concern right now.

'There's Jack to consider now, too.'

'Jack's going to be bouncing around in a day or two. Probably with a nice new cast on his arm.' Tori leaned closer to the bed she was pushing. 'What colour do you want for your arm, Jack?'

'What colours are there?'

'The whole rainbow,' Tori assured him. 'Green and blue and yellow and red. Pink, even.'

'I don't want pink.'

'Fair enough. You shall have whatever colour you want, Jack. You deserve it for being so brave.' Her glance at Matt was mischievous. 'Uncle Matt's being quite brave as well.' She lowered her voice. 'So you deserve what you want, too.'

'And what is it that I want?' Matt knew quite well where this was leading, but he was enjoying the look on Tori's face so much he wanted to spin it out just a little longer.

'Some fun,' Tori answered firmly. 'In paradise. With me,' she added with a grin that suggested she was the best part of the deal.

And Matthew found himself grinning back. He knew

his parents would cope for a day or two, even with a small boy with his arm in a cast and a sulky teenager. The lure of the short holiday *was* irresistible.

Or was it Victoria Preston who was irresistible?

CHAPTER FIVE

'WANT some company?'

Tori could only nod. If she'd tried to speak, her words would have caught on that lump in her throat. Had Matt sensed the peculiar loneliness that had brought her out to sit in the tropical warmth of this Fijian night? His smile suggested that he knew exactly how she felt, and his words confirmed it.

'Bit hard to sleep and let go of such a perfect day, isn't it?'

Tori could smile now. And speak. 'It was, wasn't it?' She drew in a deep breath and exhaled slowly. 'Just perfect.'

'It's only 1 a.m. Kind of early to pack up a wedding party.' Matt sat down carefully on the wicker swing seat Tori was curled up on, but the gentle rocking the weight of his body caused was pleasant rather than intrusive.

'The boats needed to travel together for safety in the dark.' Tori's smile wobbled just a little. 'And pregnant brides need their rest.'

'It was a beautiful wedding.'

'Mmm.' Tori closed her eyes for a moment, letting images drift. Love and laughter had permeated far more than the ceremony on the beach and Sarah had been glowing with far more than impending motherhood. Her long, dark hair had flowed loose over the simple white dress, her feet had been bare and the garland of tropical flowers in her hair the only adornment she had needed. Tori's eyes opened slowly but her tone was dreamy. 'Sarah looked gorgeous, didn't she?'

'So did you. Did you know that Sarah had chosen a dress for you in exactly the same shade of blue as your eyes?'

'No.' Tori looked away quickly. Fabric that matched eye colour wasn't the sort of thing a friend would notice, was it? Especially a *male* friend. But, then, she had admired the way Matt's open-necked cream shirt had darkened his skin and hair, hadn't she? And while she had dismissed Sarah's rather meaningful glance at one point, she had been aware of an odd pride at having provided such a good-looking member of the wedding party.

Matt had fitted in so well with the small group as well. They'd only arrived the night before the wedding but nobody would guess they hadn't all known each other for years. The beer-drinking session that had gone on long after Sarah and Tori had both gone to bed had been all Ben had seemed to need in the way of a stag night, and when Ben had asked Matt only this morning if he would act as his best man, it had seemed the wedding party's completion had been pre-ordained.

'I've never seen a bride who was both barefoot *and* pregnant.' Matt sounded amused. 'Just as well I didn't say that in my speech, though, eh?'

Tori's smile faded a little too quickly. 'She's so happy.' She caught Matt's gaze and then wished she hadn't. He saw too much. It was selfish to feel left out. Or envious.

'You haven't lost her, you know,' Matt said gently. 'You've just gained some more family. Ben's a nice guy and Phoebe's a real treat.'

Tori nodded. 'You'd never know that Phoebe wasn't

Sarah's daughter now. They're a real family, aren't they?'

'And you're part of it. Phoebe thinks her new aunty is wonderful, and you'll be seeing a lot more of them all soon. From what Ben was saying last night, it looks as though they'll be able to shift to New Zealand well before the baby arrives.'

In the short silence that followed, Tori stared at her bare feet, wiggling toes that had their nails painted a soft shell pink. She could feel Matt's gaze resting on her skin and it gave her an odd sensation, like an unexpected puff of a breeze. She wiggled her toes a little more quickly.

'They're very lucky, aren't they?' Matt murmured a little wistfully. 'To have found each other.'

'Mmm.'

So Matt was feeling the same way she was. To witness the love and commitment that had joined the lives of Sarah and Ben today had been the kind of fairy-tale ending to a search everybody made at some point in their lives. And they *were* very lucky. How many people found the right person at the right time and knew that their love was strong enough to overcome any obstacle and last the distance?

Matt was in a position where it was almost impossible to continue that search and, maybe as a result of the ceremony she had witnessed only today, Tori had just woken up to the yearning that made simply having fun seem like a waste of time. In the midst of all the joy of the wedding, they had both been left with a sense of personal sadness. Of being left out.

It seemed an automatic gesture to offer comfort, and the seat rocked again a little as Tori reached out and touched Matt's arm. She had intended to say something along the lines of the right person being out there wait-ing for him, but the jolt of some weird kind of elec-tricity on her fingertips was disconcerting. That wasn't something that should happen between friends either, was it? Tori pulled her hand back and any words of comfort died on her lips.

Matt looked momentarily startled as well. He turned his attention sharply to the view from the small balcony they shared, and seemed only too keen to change the subject.

'Gorgeous view, isn't it? I love the way the moon-light catches ripples in the water. And there's so many islands out there, all looking dark and mysterious.'

'This island is the best. I don't think I'll ever want to go anywhere else for a holiday. And that rock pool on the beach just had to be the most romantic spot on earth for a wedding. I'm so glad it didn't rain.'

'I don't think Sarah or Ben would have noticed if it had.'

'The guests might have. And it would have spoiled that wonderful island-style feast they did in the gar-den.'

'Speaking of guests, I feel a bit bad that I'm the only one who gets to stay here.'

'I'm the closest relative,' Tori reminded him. 'Apart from that elderly aunt of Ben's, and if she'd been given the guest bure bed, we would both have been camping on the couch.'

The look they exchanged was even more discon-certing than that touch on Matt's arm had been, and Tori felt her heart rate pick up noticeably. There was more than a flicker of interest burning in the depths of those hazel eyes, undoubtedly prompted by the sug-gestion of shared sleeping quarters.

Tori swallowed hard. This was definitely not something that should happen between friends, and right now was not a good time to ponder just how undeniable Matt Buchanan's physical attractions were.

They were, to all intents and purposes, alone. Tucked away in the velvety, warm tropical darkness in a small guest suite that was separated from both the main house and housekeeper's quarters. They were sitting close together and were barely dressed.

Tori was wearing silk boxer shorts and the soft singlet top she preferred to sleep in. Matt was also wearing boxer shorts. He had thrown on that cream shirt he had been wearing earlier today before coming outside, but he hadn't bothered to button it. Tori could see the glow of sun-kissed skin on his chest, which was only lightly dusted with tawny hair.

'Most of the guests were local anyway,' she added hurriedly. 'Ben's got to know a lot of people by working here.' It wasn't that she could see that glowing bare skin on Matt's chest in the dim light. It was more that she could *feel* it. Maybe it was time she yawned or something and excused herself to go to bed.

The thought of the empty, queen-sized bed in the room just behind her made Tori's mouth feel suddenly dry. It refused to co-operate by faking a yawn. And Matt was staring at her with an odd expression.

'Nasoya worked at the island resort Sas and I stayed at last year. I never knew he could play a guitar that well, though. Wasn't the singing fabulous? And you know that cute little Fijian girl that was helping Phoebe scatter petals? Her name's Milika, and Sarah actually saved her from drowning. Sas is practically an adopted member of that village now...' Tori's prattle faded on noticing Matt's teeth gleaming as he grinned.

'What? What's so funny?'

'I'm not laughing,' he protested. 'I'm just enjoying listening to you talk. You enjoy everything so much, it's contagious.' His smile was almost poignant. 'I feel very lucky to be here and I'm very glad you're my friend.'

'Well, I'm lucky, too.' Tori tore her gaze away from the warmth in Matt's hazel eyes, but it didn't seem to help to focus on his hands. Strong-looking hands with long fingers that looked capable of being very sensitive. They were resting on an even longer stretch of bare thigh. It was almost impossible to keep her tone as light as she had intended. 'Not many people would put up with me talking so much, but I feel like I can say anything to you.'

'You can. I really like listening.'

For a short time there was nothing for Matt to listen to as Tori closed her eyes firmly and really tried to squash the awareness she had of Matt's body right now. It was Matt's quiet voice that broke the silence.

'I really like you, Tori.'

'I like you, too, Matt.'

'I just wish…'

'What?' Tori snorted softly. 'That I didn't talk so much?'

'No.'

'What, then?' She knew perfectly well where this was heading. Where she *hoped* this was heading? The safe thing to do here would be to back off. Fast. She had yet another opportunity to do so when Matt cleared his throat but said nothing. She didn't, though. Something was pulling at Tori. Something far too strong to resist.

'Matt?'

'Your friendship means a lot to me,' Matt said reluctantly. 'There's no one else that would really understand how difficult my life is right now. I can whinge or joke about the kids and know that you're not going to take it the wrong way. And you were right. Hayley backed down when I told her I was coming away for a couple of days, and that was that. She sulked and slammed a door or two but I got the impression she respected me for standing my ground.'

'Of course she did. They're all great kids, Matt, and I'm sure Hayley, more than any of the others, realises that what you're doing for them all is amazing. *I* couldn't do it, which means you're a better person than me.' Tori grinned. 'There you go—you're a good influence.'

Matt gave a huff of laughter. 'Yeah…right. I'm just waiting for my good influence to get you out on the road full time as an ambulance officer. You're brilliant, Tori. Joe thinks so, too. We both love working with you.'

'I'm getting around to it. I've made some enquiries about cross-crediting my nursing qualifications. When I get that sorted, I'll just have to put in a month's notice at the ED.'

Matt didn't seem to be listening. 'The problem is that I like being around you a bit too much, Tori. Right now, I feel I'm being dishonest if I don't warn you that I'm very attracted to you. I thought I had it under control but being with you here, like this, makes me realise just how much I've been kidding myself.'

'Oh…' She'd asked for this, hadn't she? She'd seen it coming and had practically jumped up and down, waving the finish flag. The question was, what was she going to do about it now? Her mouth seemed to have it sorted. It opened again with absolutely no conscious effort. 'I...I'm attracted to you, too, Matt.'

They stared at each other. Somehow their hands had found each other in the small gap between them. They touched and held in much the same way as their lines of vision had. An intense eye contact that went on...and on. Matt's thumb was moving in slow circles on Tori's palm and the movement sent spirals of sensation through her body, so utterly delicious it made her pink-tipped toes curl. When Matt finally spoke he didn't let go of her hand or look away.

'What do you want to do about that, Tori?'

'I...um...' Tori didn't want to tell Matt what she wanted to do about it. Would he think less of her if she offered sex with no strings? It was important that he didn't think less of her. Maybe important enough to be able to ignore the fierce desire rocking her world at this point.

'I don't know,' she admitted. The sensations she was experiencing here were enough to curdle some very basic rules she had put in place in her life. Boundaries were simply evaporating and she couldn't have cared less. 'What do *you* want to do about it?'

The intoxicating spirals of pleasure slowed and then stopped as Matt dragged his gaze away and stared out to sea, but he still held her hand. Or was she holding his? Tori saw muscles in Matt's neck constrict as he swallowed. His mouth opened but then closed wordlessly, and for the longest time there were simply the sounds of the night.

A rustle as some creature moved in the undergrowth nearby. The croak of what sounded like a frog and even the gentle wash of waves on the beach well below the bure. And then Matt sighed and any background noises vanished as Tori waited, her heart hammering, for him to speak.

'I don't want to lose your friendship,' he said. 'If we made love, it would change things.'

'It…it might give us a closer friendship.' The shaft of disappointment cut deep. Tori had to fight an urge to still Matt's words by covering his lips with her fingers. No…make that with her own lips.

'We both know there can't be a future for us.' Matt sounded completely resigned. 'I understand and accept your reasons for not wanting to take on someone else's children. I would probably feel exactly the same way if I'd grown up in your situation.'

Matt paused to take in a deep, slow breath. It was a moment that Tori could have used to deny that absolute exclusion she had set for her future. She could admit that seeing Sarah with Phoebe today had made her wonder just how valid her criteria were. But something held her back. Maybe it was the knowledge of how different Sarah was to herself. How different her foster-sister's perspective was. Sas had been the one who had come in from the outside. She had been the one receiving the gift of a family, not the one who had had to give it. Having Matt with her had been enough to dismiss that flash of doubt. Enough to remind her of the night in that dreadful garage. Of Charlene and Monique and the kind of damage that was possible by opening one's life to children in need.

And while her heart and body were doing a very effective job of trying to wipe out the arguments that put Matt Buchanan firmly out of bounds right now, a part of Tori's head was sounding some very clear alarm bells. She couldn't deny Matt's statement. There *was* no future for them. Not long term. But why did that mean they couldn't enjoy what they could have? A close friendship. A *very* close friendship.

'Having a physical relationship would make us more than friends,' Matt continued softly. 'And one of us would end up getting hurt. I might find it impossible not to fall in love with you and then where would I be?' His hand squeezed Tori's as his breath came out in a huff of wry laughter. 'My life is complicated enough right now.'

Again Tori said nothing. This time it was because she was struggling with disappointment that was almost enough to bring her to tears. He was right. It would be Matt that ended up getting more hurt and it would be selfish to demand what she wanted from him more than anything right now. *She* had set the boundaries and that part of her head that was sounding the alarm made her only too aware how unfair it would be to suggest that those boundaries could be adjusted for the moment.

It wasn't as if they were going to go away. Maybe it would have been different if Matt had just had a little girl—like Phoebe. But he didn't. He had *four* children, and one of them was an unhappy teenager who reminded her, a shade too closely, of Monique.

'It's probably just the setting that's done this.' Matt sounded as though he was trying to convince himself as much as Tori. 'We've spent the day watching two people who are totally in love with each other get married. Weddings are notorious for sparking things off among guests anywhere, but we've done it in what has to be the most romantic spot on earth.'

His thumb was doing that circle thing again on Tori's palm. She should pull away before the frustration drove her totally crazy, but she couldn't bring herself to break the contact.

'It's made us both feel a bit lonely,' Matt continued. 'We like each other...a lot. And we've been left to our own devices.' He paused and swallowed noticeably again. 'It would be very, very easy to get carried away here.'

Tori looked up to catch Matt's gaze and she had to bite her lip to prevent interrupting him. It would be more than easy. What was going to be impossibly difficult was *not* to get *carried away*.

'If we did, I suspect that one or both of us would regret it as soon as we got home and back to reality,' Matt continued relentlessly. 'And that would end up destroying our friendship.' With a final squeeze, Matt let go of Tori's hand. 'And I'm not going to let that happen.'

He stood up, the seat rocking violently enough to almost tip Tori onto the floor. Matt caught her shoulders and slowed the movement. Then he leaned down and kissed her, very lightly, on her lips.

'Goodnight, Tori.' His voice was as soft a caress as his lips had been. Almost not there but strangely it could be felt strongly enough to be almost painful. 'Sleep well.'

This *wasn't* her fault!

It was inevitable that Matt would catch Tori's gaze as he entered Resus 1. It had become a reflex action on her part to look up whenever she caught a glimpse of an ambulance service uniform coming into the emergency department and if it *was* Matt, he was always looking back.

The unspoken messages in those looks had changed steadily over the last ten days—ever since they had returned from attending Sarah's wedding in Fiji—and this time there was no escaping the fact that Matt was feeling hurt.

But it *wasn't* Tori's fault.

For heaven's sake, she was doing the right thing here, wasn't she? The only thing she could be doing, given that reality hadn't altered the way she felt about Matt one iota. She wanted more than a conventional friendship with this man.

She wanted *him*, dammit!

It had been hard work, hiding it, but she wasn't going to force herself on him. Yes, making love would change things between them, but *not* making love was having its own damaging effect and it was becoming easier to avoid the frustration by simply avoiding Matt. Yes, one or both of them could end up being hurt but wasn't that the case in any relationship? Tori was prepared to take the risk but it was Matt who was less willing to complicate his life any further and, yes, she had to concede that it was Matt who had more to lose and therefore it had to be his decision.

Tori had had no intention of forcing the issue by cancelling the shift she had booked on the road as an observer for her day off yesterday, but the disturbed sleep of the night before, punctuated by all-too-vivid dreams, had made avoidance of a whole day with the object of her desire more than prudent.

And now Matt was offended. Probably feeling rejected and hurt.

Not that he let it show by anything more than a split second of eye contact with Tori. The stretcher was being wheeled swiftly into the most high-tech of the resuscitation areas that was kept available, if at all possible, for status one medical patients.

'This is Martin Burns,' Matt told the doctor leading

the team. 'He's thirty-two years old and has no known medical history. He presented with sudden onset "ripping" chest pain, radiating to his back.'

The patient was unusually tall. His feet protruded from the blankets to hang over the end of a stretcher that could comfortably accommodate a person at least six feet tall. He was also very thin. Tori wondered if he had yet to be diagnosed with a connective tissue disorder such as Marfan's syndrome. Her curiosity was enough to distract Tori from the wash of Matt's voice as she positioned herself to help transfer the patient to the bed.

'On arrival, blood pressure was 180 over 75 in his left arm, 150 over 65 in his right arm.'

Tori glanced up at the consultant, hoping he was looking as impressed as he should. How many paramedics would recognise that this chest pain was more indicative of an aortic dissection than, say, a heart attack? Or would check the blood pressure on both arms to find the classic sign of inequality?

'Pain level is down to 5 out of 10 after 15 milligrams of morphine.'

'Ready?' The leader of the medical team was at the head end of the stretcher and had taken hold of the loosened sheet covering the stretcher mattress. 'One, two...three!'

The transfer of the patient was smooth. Tori was ready with the ECG leads and Matt flicked off the electrodes that were still attached to the portable monitor. She smiled at the anxious-looking young man.

'Hi, Martin. You're doing well. Don't worry about all these wires. We just need to run a few tests.'

'Rhythm has been sinus and steady at 80,' Matt was saying.

He had felt their fingers brush in passing as they'd changed electrodes. Tori could tell by the infinitesimal tightening of his tone. 'Lungs are clear, respiration rate of 20. Oxygen saturation 98 per cent on 8 litres of oxygen.'

Tori took the end of the oxygen tubing as Matt pulled it from the portable cylinder.

'Thanks, Matt.' She reached up to plug it onto the overhead oxygen port for the resus area. A task she wouldn't normally fumble over, but the glance she had caught from Matt was unsettling. They needed to talk but a busy emergency department was hardly the place and Matt didn't have the time any more than she did. Tori could recognise the sound his pager was making that heralded another priority-one callout.

Joe was already halfway out the door with the stretcher.

'Good job. Thanks, Matt.' The emergency consultant's appreciation was as fleeting as the paramedic's remaining presence in the room. He was signalling one of his registrars. 'Get hold of Cardiology,' he told her. 'We need a transoesophageal echo, stat.'

There was no more of an opportunity forty-five minutes later when Matt and Joe returned from the callout with a teenage girl who had fractured her pelvis, falling off a galloping horse.

This was a real emergency. The body splint was probably not doing much to reduce the internal bleeding and it was possible to lose enough blood to go into irreversible hypovolaemic shock or even bleed out very quickly because of the major vessels the injury could have affected.

The girl already had two large-bore IV cannulae in

place, with fluids pouring in, but she was pale, sweaty and vomiting and her blood pressure was still dropping. Tori barely saw Matt come or go. More IV sites were needed with rapid transfusion cannulae. Type-matching for blood was a priority but other blood products were used in the interim. Injuries other than the pelvic fracture had to be identified and dealt with as quickly as possible, and then an urgent orthopaedic consult was demanded for the external fixation the fracture needed.

By the time this patient had been stabilised and Tori returned from having accompanied her to Theatre, Matt had been and gone with another patient. It had been Maureen who had apparently answered the questions he'd had about Martin Burns and had been able to tell him that it was a type B dissection, distal to the left subclavian artery, and could be managed medically without urgent surgical intervention.

'He was really pleased to hear that,' Maureen told Tori smugly. 'We talked about it for ages.'

Despite wanting to avoid hearing any more of Maureen's conversation with Matt, and even after the clock showed she had gone past the time her shift was due to finish at 5 p.m., Tori took her time handing over her remaining patients and even had a coffee in the staffroom, hoping for a chance to talk to Matt. In the end she had to admit defeat, however, and she climbed into her ancient car, waited for the engine to warm up to its familiar and comforting rumble and then she headed away from the hospital and the city.

Away from any chance to see Matt again that day.

Maybe it was for the best, anyway. Talking to Matt was going to be difficult. He knew she was avoiding him. Maybe he also knew why. Tori hoped he didn't feel hurt because he'd decided she thought his friendship was no longer enough for her. After all, the prime reason he had given for not wanting to extend their relationship into a physical realm was because he didn't want to risk losing their friendship.

And that was precisely what was going to happen the way things were going.

And that *was* her fault. She was the one avoiding spending time with him just because it was easier.

As soon as she left the motorway for a quieter stretch of road, Tori pulled over, switched off the loud music and retrieved her cellphone from her bag. Matt's number was easy to find but it proved a lot harder to make the call. What if he was so offended he didn't want to talk to her? Or what if he was in the middle of a late job and couldn't talk?

Thank goodness for text messaging. It took only seconds.

'Miss U,' she sent.

The beep of her phone as a return message came through sent a curious thrill through Tori and she pressed her 'OK' button eagerly.

'Me 2,' Matt had sent.

The prickle of tears was totally unexpected. Tori hadn't realised just how *much* she was missing Matt's company until she had received the reassurance. She blinked hard as the phone beeped again.

'U busy 2nite?'

Did he want to see her? To talk? Tori wanted that, too. Badly. It didn't matter that there couldn't be any more to their relationship. She just wanted to see Matt. To be with him and enjoy his company. There were so many things she wanted to tell him—like the fact that a piece of land with a lovely modern house on it had come for sale just up the coast from her own home and that Ben and Sarah were excited about the possibility of purchasing it. And she wanted to know about the job they had done with Martin Burns today. How Matt had picked that it was an aortic dissection and how stressful it had been to manage. And...

Her fingers were moving at the same speed the thoughts were flashing through her head.

'No,' she sent back. 'R U?'

'U @ home?'

'Soon.'

'8pm OK?'

Was he planning to *visit*? Tori caught and held her breath for a moment. They'd never visited each other's homes. In fact, the only space they'd really shared that hadn't been professional had been the guest house on Ben and Sarah's island. And look what had almost happened there!

What would happen on a warm spring evening a bit north of Auckland, New Zealand? In the isolated house where Tori now lived completely alone?

If Matt intended keeping a physical distance, it would be the last place to suggest meeting, wouldn't it?

Tori couldn't swallow. Her mouth felt far too dry. Her fingers actually shook a little as she pressed enough keys to send back a single word.

'Sure.'

CHAPTER SIX

'YOU'VE been avoiding me.'

'No, I haven't.'

'*Tori!*'

Her laughter was a delighted gurgle. 'You sound just like Sas when *she's* growling at me!' Tori had heard the tyres of Matt's car crunching over the gravel driveway and was standing at the top of the verandah steps to welcome her visitor. She sobered as Matt climbed the steps. 'Yeah,' she admitted. 'I guess I have been avoiding you. Sorry.'

Matt stopped but he was already up the steps, close enough for Tori to feel that warmth—that astonishing glow from skin despite the fact that it was perfectly well covered by more than one layer of clothing at the moment. Matt wasn't smiling.

'*Why*, Tori?'

'I...um...' A list of glib excuses sprang to mind but had to be instantly dismissed. The light wasn't great out here on the verandah, probably due to the layer of dead moths in the bowl of the outside light fitting, but Matt's brow was creased and there was no escaping the mixture of bewilderment and pain in his eyes. He deserved nothing less than the truth.

'I haven't been able to forget that night in Fiji, Matt,' she told him quietly. 'It...it hasn't gone away.'

'It?'

Tori's heart gave a painful thump that left her feeling

vaguely dizzy. The words might be screaming in her head but they were *so* hard to form with her tongue.

'Wanting you,' she whispered.

'Oh…*God*!' With a groan, Matt pulled Tori into his arms and held her tightly. His face was pressed against her hair and his next words were rather muffled. 'I feel the same way but I thought you'd decided you were better off not having me in your life. It's been hell.'

Tori tightened the hold she had around Matt's body. She could feel the outline of rigid muscles beneath the coarse wool of his jersey.

'I didn't want you to feel you were being pushed into something you didn't want. The complications, you know? And I didn't trust myself to be around you without making it too obvious what I wanted.'

'I want it just as much as you do.' Matt pulled back far enough for her to see his face.

Any thoughts Tori had had of showing Matt around her house and property, telling him of the advantages of having the beach just down the road or a border of native bush reserve, were long gone. Where they were was insignificant. They could still be on a Fijian island. They could be on the moon for all it mattered. Nothing existed apart from the two of them.

Nothing at all.

'What are we going to do?'

Matt's eyes had her pinned. What she saw in their depths fanned the curious clutch of sensation in her belly and her skin started to tingle. Tori had never felt so…*alive*.

'We're damned if we do,' Matt said softly, 'but we're damned if we *don't*.'

'Maybe we could make it work,' Tori whispered back.

'You mean, no strings for you?'

'*Or* you. Just friends…having fun.'

'And to hell with any fallout?'

Tori's face tilted as she leaned imperceptibly closer to Matt. 'Fun's important, Matt. You need some fun in your life. I thought that the first time I met you again. Why don't we just go with the flow and see what happens?'

Matt's eyes were fixed on Tori's lips as she spoke. Then he closed his eyes briefly. He muttered something about having absolutely no choice, really, but his words were barely audible and it couldn't have mattered less because his lips met Tori's even before he had finished speaking.

The first touch was feather-light. They drew apart, caught each other's gaze for a nano-second and this time when their lips met, there was no holding back. No tentative searching to find whether this was what they both really wanted. The answers were already there, like blazing neon signs.

Tori barely registered being edged backwards until her spine met the hard wooden frame around her front door. The support was all she needed to focus completely on the man she wanted so much—the exquisite pressure of his lips, the glide of his tongue, the tantalisingly sharp tendrils of pleasure his hands were providing as they moved down from cradling her head over her shoulders and arms—his thumbs brushing her breasts.

It took only the movement of raising her arms to slide her fingers into Matt's hair and hold his head even closer for his hands to fall naturally and actually cup her breasts. And now his thumbs were doing that spiral thing over her nipples and Tori knew she had never wanted anyone this much. She pressed closer with the length of her body but the sharp edge of the doorframe was there again almost instantly as Matt pressed back.

His hands dropped to find the hem of her sweatshirt and then they moved upwards again, this time on bare skin, and Tori groaned aloud. She could feel the firm outline of one of his thighs between her legs and the other firm outline she could feel let Tori know that her level of need was reciprocated here. With a huge effort she pulled her mouth away from Matt's and gulped for air.

'Come inside,' she managed. 'I want to show you my house.'

'I don't want to see your house right now,' Matt growled. 'Later.'

Tori grinned. 'But I was going to show you upstairs first. I've got clean sheets on my—'

Her sentence ended in a surprised squeak as she found herself swept up into Matt's arms. He pushed the front door open with his foot.

'Which way?' he demanded.

Tori was nuzzling his neck, thoroughly enjoying the new experience of being literally carried away. 'Try the stairs,' she murmured. 'Then it's first on the left.'

She had changed the sheets on her bed as soon as she'd arrived home after the text conversation with Matt. She had also ignored the thought of any fire risk in an old wooden house and had lit at least a dozen candles, which were perched on various surfaces around her room. If Matt realised that she had been expecting this scenario he didn't seem to mind but, then, he was too busy undressing Tori and covering each newly bared piece of skin with his hands and his lips.

Wanting to return the favour, Tori helped Matt pull his jersey over his head and remove the T-shirt he was wearing underneath. Her lips skimmed that golden skin and her tongue teased the tiny, brown nipples. But when she carefully undid the stud on his jeans and exposed a new focus for her questing hands and mouth, Matt reached down and lifted her effortlessly higher.

'I want you,' he groaned. 'I don't think I can wait.'

And Tori simply smiled, rolling onto her back and pulling Matt so that he knelt between her legs. 'Neither can I,' she breathed.

It didn't matter that their foreplay had lasted only minutes. Not this time, anyway. They had waited far too long for what should have happened that night in Fiji. Their love-making was hungry, appetites honed by frustration and self-denial, and even the mind-blowing climaxes they both reached were not enough. Not this time, anyway.

The quiet time, bathed in flickering candlelight, lying entangled in each other's limbs on top of the bed they hadn't bothered turning back, gave them the chance to start again. Gentle, long kisses this time, with space to murmur their appreciation and admiration for what they had just experienced and what they fully intended to experience again.

The candles had burned well down by the time the lovers' conversation could include anything beyond themselves and the space they were in. It was Tori who summoned the energy to break the spell.

'What time do you need to get back home?'

'I told Mum I'd be back by midnight. What time is it now?'

Tori reluctantly rolled away from the circle of Matt's

arms to find the bedside clock. '11 p.m.,' she said in dismay. 'And it'll take you half an hour to get there.'

Matt pulled her closer again. 'That gives us another half an hour, then,' he said. 'Let's make the most of it.'

Tori kissed him back. 'Does your mother know where you are?'

'I think she might have guessed. I've been like a bear with a sore head around the kids the last few days. She's been giving me funny looks ever since I came back from Fiji.'

'I'm sorry, Matt. I didn't want to make life any more complicated for you.'

'You've given me something that's worth any complications.' Matt kissed her again and Tori smiled under his lips.

'Fun?'

'The best. Do we get to do it again?'

'You bet. You weren't the only one having fun here, mate.'

'When?' The careful word couldn't hide an eagerness that Tori knew quite well belied any casual value put on what had happened between them.

'Soon,' she suggested firmly. The fact that 'no strings' was a joke, considering they might have just bound themselves together with something that resembled a shipping rope, was easy enough to shove to the back of her mind. Tori even managed to sound perfectly casual. 'It's up to you, Matt. I don't have any ties. When I'm not at work, I'm available.'

The tiny silence acknowledged Matt's weight of responsibilities. A family environment he couldn't afford to neglect. The reason that any 'strings' would have to be ignored.

'I'm working the next two nights but two of my days off are at the weekend. I could ask Mum to babysit again on one of the evenings.'

'Would she mind?'

'I think she will be quite delighted if I tell her why. She was very taken with you the day we came to the emergency department with Jack.'

'Hayley wasn't.' Tori could well remember the glaring antagonism to which she had been subjected. 'She won't be too impressed if she finds out you're coming to visit me.'

'So she won't find out,' Matt said calmly. 'I'm entitled to *some* life of my own, aren't I?'

Tori smiled. 'I'm not going to argue with that. Maybe next time I'll be able to show you my house properly.'

'Maybe.' Matt finally moved to retrieve his scattered clothes but he came back almost immediately to plant another soft kiss on Tori's lips. 'Wouldn't guarantee it, though.'

The tour of Tori's house and garden became a standing joke. Matt would turn up whenever he could snatch a few hours to himself over the next few weeks and knock on her door.

'I've come to see the house,' he would say with a remarkably straight face. 'Maybe the garden as well.'

'Of course,' Tori would respond. 'Do come in.'

Matt did get to know pockets of the rambling old house very well. The homely and rather cluttered kitchen where it was easy to rustle up a quick meal of something like scrambled eggs or delve into the creaking, antique refrigerator that was fortunately still capable of chilling a bottle of wine.

The small lounge close to the kitchen with its gas fire and the soft, old couch that held two people so comfortably.

The upstairs bathroom with its blue and white mosaic floor and a shower with dodgy plumbing that meant you had to stand very close together if you both wanted to stay remotely warm.

Best of all, though, Matt knew every corner of the big bedroom that was Tori's. If he was there during any daylight hours, the view from the second-storey window was a delight, with native forest to one side of the garden and just a glimpse of sea towards the front. The view inside the room was even more enticing, with the rich glow of polished timber flooring, the pretty russet and white tiles of the fireplace and a battered, scotch chest that barely had room for the fat scented candles amongst the collection of Tori's childhood treasures and general feminine debris.

The house was a bit like Tori, in fact. Not particularly tidy, with generous curves and a warmth that made you feel as though you had arrived home. It didn't matter that there were areas Matt hadn't yet glimpsed. What he had seen was more than enough to keep him firmly hooked, and the promise of discovering more was a pleasure he was quite happy to keep postponing.

It gave him an excuse to keep visiting, didn't it? And yet another private joke that added to the wonderful closeness of his friendship with this woman. Except that it didn't end up being much of a joke the night he *did* get to see a new area of the old house.

The wild weather had gone unnoticed in the time he and Tori had just spent in each other's arms. Hail and rain battering the corrugated iron of the roof and wind that rattled the glass panes of the windows and made the candle flames dance in odd drafts had provided a fitting background to the stormy passion inside the room.

Matt was still trying to catch his breath as he became aware of the strength of the southerly blast outside. He pulled Tori a little closer to his body and reached for the duvet to cover them both. She snuggled against him with a sound like a contented cat and Matt pressed a kiss into her blonde curls.

'You're amazing, you know that?'

'You're not so dusty yourself, mate.'

Matt smiled into the darkness. He couldn't say what he really thought. This was supposed to be fun, wasn't it? Casual. If he confessed to Tori that they shared the most amazing sex he had ever had the pleasure of experiencing, that he could never, ever get enough of it, she might feel trapped. Obliged to stick around when a better offer came along even. An offer that didn't have unwanted dependants attached.

And he certainly couldn't tell her that perhaps the most magic moments were these—when he got to hold her in his arms like this after they had made love. When the closeness they had was more than he had ever felt with another human being and it made him feel complete. Invincible even.

No, he could say nothing. All he could do was enjoy the moment, and possibly convey just a small part of what he felt through the occasional touch of his lips on her hair or the brush of his fingertips along a portion of that gloriously soft skin. The fact that it could never be permanent made it all the more precious. And poignant.

Not that it ever lasted all that long anyway. The irrepressible Tori would twist in his arms all too soon. To inflame passion again if they had the luxury of time or maybe to suggest a shower or say she was 'absolutely *starving*' and why didn't they go and cook a bacon sandwich or something?

But this time there was no mischievous glint in the eyes that flew open and the tension Matt could feel in her body had nothing to do with passion.

'Oh, my God! What was *that*?'

The cracking noise had been disconcerting. It had been way too close for it to have been a branch coming down from a tree. 'It's the wind,' Matt decided, when only the pelt of heavy raindrops could be heard after the gust. 'It's OK now.'

The next vicious gust made it all too apparent that things weren't OK, however. The banging sound from above their heads was too loud to ignore.

'The roof's coming off,' Tori said in horror.

'Let's find a torch.' Matt was pulling his clothes on rapidly. 'I'll take a look.'

Driving sheets of rain made it difficult to see much at all, but the sound of the flapping sheet of corrugated iron let Matt at least make some kind of assessment.

'It only seems to be one sheet,' he told Tori. 'The nails were probably a bit loose already and the wind has lifted a corner. Let's check the other side of the house while we're out here.'

They were both soaked and freezing by the time they trudged back inside. Tori had found an old oilskin coat for Matt to wear but his jeans were decidedly the worse for wear.

'You'd better have a shower and warm up,' she told him. 'I'll put your jeans in the dryer. Hayley's going to think you had a rather odd night out with Joe at the pub if you go home this wet.'

Matt came out of the bathroom to find Tori in the upstairs hallway with her arms full of pots.

'What the—?'

'The roof's leaking,' she told him. 'There's a water-fall going right into my bed!'

'Oh…no!' Matt helped Tori shove furniture around in her room and position pots. She stared with dismay at the stains appearing on her ceiling.

'This is awful,' she wailed. 'What am I going to do?'

'The storm's supposed to blow out tonight,' Matt said. 'There's nothing you can do outside right now anyway. You'll need to call someone tomorrow to come and fix it.'

'But it's Sunday tomorrow. Even if I could find any-one, they'll charge an arm and a leg!'

Matt frowned. 'Is the money a problem for you, Tori?'

She nodded miserably. 'Mum left Sarah and me the house and it hasn't got a mortgage on it, but that was it. With Sarah to help share the costs like electricity, we've managed OK, but there's never been any left over for stuff like maintenance, which is probably why the roof's falling apart now.'

They both looked at the drip forming on a new patch of ceiling. It rapidly collected water and plopped onto the wooden floor. Tori grabbed the last empty pot and positioned it. A new drip landed with a musical 'ping' and her bottom lip wobbled.

'I don't know how I'm going to afford this,' she said quietly. 'It's a disaster. We probably need a whole new roof.'

The wobbly lip did something strange to Matt. With

a feeling something like he got when the twins fell over and needed attention, he wrapped his arms around Tori and made soothing noises.

'It'll be OK, babe. You won't need a whole new roof. That bit of iron just needs nailing down, and if the other nails are looked at it probably won't happen again. It's no big deal. I could do it myself.'

'Could you?' Tori's eyes shone with unshed tears and a small ray of hope. 'Really?'

'Sure. I could come out tomorrow if you like.' Matt couldn't help sounding slightly dubious. 'I'd have to bring the kids, though. I can't ask Mum to babysit again. She really needs a whole day off.'

'Not a problem,' Tori said quickly. 'Oh, Matt! If you could help fix my roof, it would be *wonderful*!'

'Consider it done.' Matt pushed aside any nervousness about bringing the children here and pushing them into Tori's life. This was an emergency. Tori needed his help and he would do anything it took. 'I'll pick up some new roofing nails on the way and we'll be out here by about 9 a.m. if the rain's stopped. Will that do?'

Tori's answer was by way of a very enthusiastic kiss. 'You're an angel, Matt. I love you!'

Gleeful cries of children were a sound that had not echoed within Tori's living space for many years but, far from being annoying, it was surprisingly enjoyable.

It was just that she was so pleased to have Matt coming to her rescue that nothing would be irritating, Tori decided. Or maybe it was because the storm had blown itself out overnight, leaving the freshest blue sky and a lovely smell of damp earth in the garden.

'Sorry, it's a bit wet out here. I haven't had a chance to cut the grass for ages.'

'You need a goat,' Matt suggested. He stepped round the longer clumps of grass that were up to his knees as they made their way to the old stables, then he eyed the cobwebs on the huge iron door latch. 'Guess you haven't used a ladder for ages either. You sure it's in here?'

'Pretty sure. There's a fair bit of junk, though.'

A troop of wide-eyed children were peering eagerly past Matt as he hauled open the tall doors.

'It's like a junk shop,' Jack yelled with delight. 'Cool!'

'Junk is right,' Hayley muttered. She stayed outside, making a point of brushing at the wet hems of her flared jeans.

'If you didn't have them dragging on the ground, they wouldn't get as wet,' Charles informed his sister. 'Hey, Tori—can we play with some of this stuff?'

'Sure.' She raised an eyebrow at Matt. 'They all up to date with their tetanus shots?'

'Watch out for rusty stuff, kids. And no bleeding, OK? I've got enough to fix up on Tori's roof.'

'This is really nice of you, Matt.' Tori cast a guilty glance towards Hayley. 'I get the impression that it wasn't a unanimously popular way to spend a Sunday.'

'It'll do her good,' Matt murmured back. 'She was all set to spend the day trawling the malls with her mates.'

'Look at *this*!' Jack had pulled aside some sacks of pine cones that were now spilling onto the cobbled floor. 'Does it still go, Tori?'

She looked at the ancient bicycle that had a basket attached to the handlebars. 'The tyres are probably a bit flat. Are you supposed to be doing things like riding a bike when your arm is still in a cast, Jack?'

'My cast comes off in three days,' Jack told her. 'It doesn't hurt at all any more—even when I do *this*!' He whacked his arm against one of the supporting posts for the stable roof. Tori winced but Matt grinned.

'I suspect that while his arm is still protected is the best time to do things like riding a bike. That is, if you're sure you don't mind, Tori.'

'This stuff has been in here since I was a kid. Look, Bonnie—there's my old doll's pram.'

'Ooh, can I see? Please?'

It was Matt who climbed over what appeared to be part of an old tractor to haul out the cane pram.

'You might find a box of old dolls and toys back there as well, Matt.'

'I thought we came in here for the ladder.'

Tori winked at Bonnie. 'Have a look for it while you're getting the pram out. It's in there somewhere.'

Charles was peering into a dust-laden shaft of sunshine illuminating a corner of the old building.

'Uncle Matt! Come and check *this* out!'

'In a minute, Charles. I need to find this ladder or we'll never get the roof fixed.'

'I think it might be a cat's skeleton. Or even a *rat*!'

Bonnie shrieked but was still close behind Jack as he went to inspect the new treasure.

'Can I have it, Tori?' Charles asked. 'For my collection?'

'Sure.' Tori was grinning broadly now. 'Be my guest.'

'Cheers.' Matt was extracting the wooden extension ladder from behind the tractor. 'Let's get out of here before they find anything else, huh?'

Tori watched anxiously, hanging on to the bottom of the ladder, as Matt went roofwards. For the next half an hour the sound of hammering echoed amongst the shouts and cheerful arguments of the children. Jack was doing his best to ride a bike that was far too big for him and had very flat tyres. Bonnie had abandoned the pram and was begging for her turn on the bike. Charles was carefully picking lumps of fur off the skeleton and Tori had to admit to being in sympathy with the expression of utmost disgust that was on Hayley's face as she watched him.

Matt made his way carefully down the ladder. 'I need the other packet of nails,' he told Tori. 'I think I've fixed the broken bit but the other nails could all do with a bang and there's quite a few missing. I'm surprised you haven't had a few more leaks upstairs.'

'How did you know the leak was upstairs?'

Tori was impressed with the way Matt managed to look totally unfazed by both Hayley's sudden appearance nearby and the innuendo in her question.

'Tori told me,' he responded casually. 'Besides, if a roof is leaking in a two-storied house, you'd expect it to be upstairs, wouldn't you?' He turned to Tori. 'Perhaps you wouldn't mind giving me a bit of a tour later. We can check for any signs of dampness on the ceilings so I'll know if there are any areas that need particular attention.'

Tori caught the gleam of amusement in his eyes but bit back her smile. Keeping things determinedly casual in front of the kids actually made secret communication rather fun. 'I'd be more than happy to give you a tour, Matt. Any time.'

The children were not going to be left out. Hayley

seemed to perk up considerably as they all trooped through her house.

'It's nearly as messy as my room, Uncle Matt.'

Tori ignored the blatant criticism. 'I'm old enough and ugly enough to ignore housework when I've got better things to do.' She did her best to avoid catching Matt's glance but she couldn't help looking in his direction when Charles spoke to her, could she? He was standing right beside his uncle after all.

'How many bedrooms have you got, Tori? This place is *huge*!'

'There's seven bedrooms and three bathrooms.'

'And about an acre of roof,' Matt added.

The twins were open-mouthed. 'Do you live here all by yourself?'

Tori nodded. 'I do now.'

'Haven't you even got a boyfriend?' Hayley picked up a candle in Tori's room and sniffed at it suspiciously. Tori waved them all towards the door, hoping that there was no evidence of Matt's recent presence in this room.

'Sure I do.' Tori was getting just a little tired of the putdowns implicit in almost everything Hayley said. 'Have you?'

Matt cleared his throat. 'Who's hungry?' he asked. 'I've brought some bread and cheese and I thought we could make some toasted sandwiches for lunch, if that's OK with Tori.'

'Sounds great.' Tori smiled at Matt. 'I'm absolutely *starving*!'

Bonnie and Jack hadn't finished interrogating Tori.

'Did you live here by yourself when you were a little girl?'

'Weren't you scared of *ghosts*?'

'No and no,' Tori responded promptly. 'Any ghosts round here would have to be friendly ones, and there were lots of people living here when I was growing up.'

'Have you got lots of brothers and sisters, then?'

'No. I was an only child, but my mum loved kids so much she fostered them.'

'What's foster?'

'She looked after children that needed help,' Matt explained. 'It's kind of like adoption but sometimes it's only for a little while. Not for ever.'

'You mean, they got sent somewhere else if they were naughty?' Bonnie looked horrified. 'You wouldn't do that to us, would you, Uncle Matt?'

Matt scooped his niece into his arms. 'You're adopted, Bonnie. So are Jack and Charles and Hayley. You're my children now. For ever and ever.' He cuddled her, kissed the top of her head and then set her down again. 'That does *not* give you licence to be as naughty as you feel like being, however.'

Hayley may have been pretending supreme indifference but Tori couldn't miss the vaguely triumphant look sent in her direction as she slid freshly toasted sandwiches onto a plate. 'He's ours,' the look told her. 'So there!'

'Fostering *can* be kind of for ever, too,' Tori told Bonnie as she poured milk into glasses for them. 'My sister Sarah didn't come to live with us until she was fourteen, but we'll always be sisters now.'

'Are you like twins?'

'Sas was a lot older than me. About as much older as Hayley is than you. She used to look after me and try and keep me out of trouble.'

'I'll bet that was hard work.' Matt shut the toaster

on some more sandwiches. 'It was Sarah that got married, Bonnie. You remember that weekend I went away just after Jack broke his arm?'

'To the island? The one with the pool on the beach?'

'That's the one.'

'Can we go there, Uncle Matt?' Jack's small round face beneath the halo of blond curls crinkled earnestly. 'I want to go swimming. Ple-e-ease?'

'I…ah…' Matt looked towards Tori, clearly needing help.

'The beaches round here are just as good for swimming,' Tori told him. 'I used to swim every day at the beach just down the road from here.'

'Oh-h!' The twins breathed out simultaneously. 'Can we go to the beach down the road, Uncle Matt?'

'Maybe in summer,' Matt said. 'It's still a bit cold to go swimming.'

'Can we come back again, Tori?' Bonnie begged. 'And ride the bike and go swimming and stuff?'

'In summer?' Jack added. 'When it's hot?'

'Sure.' Tori smiled at Matt to let him know she was quite happy with the arrangement. Summer was a long way off yet, wasn't it? It wasn't as though she was going to have the kids running riot in her house every weekend. Once in a while was perfectly all right as far as she was concerned. Just so long as they didn't start intruding on the times she had Matt all to herself.

The twins were satisfied. 'Tori's cool, isn't she, Uncle Matt?'

'You bet.' The wink Matt gave her was so subtle that Tori was sure no one else would have picked up on it.

Then she caught Hayley's expression and realised that at least one other person had. With a mental shrug

Tori smiled at the surly teenager. The shrug was followed by an equally private sigh of relief. Hayley, with her moods and insecurities, was not her problem. And never would be.

Matt had the support of his family, particularly his mother, Linda, in having at least a small part of his life to himself. An evening once a week. Twice, sometimes, if they were lucky.

Tori had compromised in the decision to change careers for the moment. Having been granted an ambulance qualification, she had made herself available for casual work, which she intended to supplement with casual work in the emergency department of the Royal. That way, she had some control over where and when she worked. She could time her days off to coincide with some of Matt's, and when she was out on the road she could choose to base herself at the same station. While they couldn't actually work on the same vehicle, they still saw a lot of each other during the day, on station or at shared jobs and when their paths crossed at the hospital.

It was enough to sustain what had become a precious friendship. A lot more than a friendship really, but Tori had no intention of letting Matt know how much he meant to her. If someone else came along who was prepared to help take on his orphanage, she certainly wouldn't stand in his way. She didn't want Matt to feel obliged to hang around if he got a better offer. She wasn't intending to hang around herself, was she? Not for ever.

They were just good friends. Really, *really* good friends. And while they had the time to enjoy each other exclusively, Tori intended to make the most of it. She was happy. More than happy. And the time they had together was more than enough.

CHAPTER SEVEN

IT WASN'T enough.

The fact that they needed expert back-up for the job they were on was not nearly enough to explain how good it was to see Matt climbing down the long ladder into a dry dock on Auckland's harbourside.

The injured man had fallen from a platform positioned for repairs on the container ship's hull and now lay like a beached whale in the depths of the dock, with a pool of blood beneath his head. A very unapproachable whale due to how combative his head injury had rendered him. Treating the victim was going to be hard enough. Trying to extricate him by winching a stretcher up at least a hundred feet of narrow cast-iron ladder would have been impossible without the sedation someone of Matt's qualifications could administer.

Seeing the arrival of any paramedic of his level would have been a relief, but the pleasure of seeing Matt was far greater. It was partly due to the fact that Tori hadn't seen him for nearly three weeks now. Well, hadn't seen him alone, anyway. Her casual employment as an ambulance officer had given her a day or two catching him in passing on station and even her reduced hours in the emergency department had allowed other, brief meetings here and there, but they hadn't had a chance for any *real* time together.

And this meeting wasn't going to provide it either. Not yet, anyway.

'He fell from that platform up there.' Tori pointed

and Matt whistled silently as his gaze scanned the rusty expanse of the ship's hull. 'GCS was about 8 when we arrived. It's gone up to 12 but we haven't been able to collar him or even assess him properly because of his combativeness.'

Tori's partner for the day, John, was a young ambulance officer whose qualifications had not yet reached her level. He was solid enough himself but had just landed a thump on his chin from the patient's fist as he'd tried, yet again, to get some oxygen on. He was rubbing his bruised jaw ruefully as Joe rescued the oxygen cylinder and put it far enough away from their patient that it couldn't become a potentially lethal weapon.

'His name's Snapper, apparently,' Tori told Matt. A corner of her mouth twitched. 'His mates tell me that he's usually not this aggressive unless he's had a few at the pub.'

A small mob of the patient's colleagues were still grouped nearby and two were attempting to restrain Snapper by hanging on to his arms.

'He's not small, is he?' Matt was assessing the situation as best he could visually. 'Let's get another couple of his mates to sit on him,' he suggested calmly. 'Once we get an IV in and some morphine or midazolam on board, we'll be right.' Matt raised an eyebrow. 'His airway doesn't sound too compromised.'

'No.' Tori caught the definite twinkle of amusement in Matt's glance. 'I've learnt a few good new swear words.'

The opportunity to try out the new words over the next ten minutes was tempting, but Snapper's mates did that for her as they attempted to keep a flailing and very beefy arm immobile for the ambulance crew. One was virtually kneeling on Snapper's shoulder in the end, and another on his hand. Matt and Tori were squeezed in between, with a tourniquet looking ridiculously small on the well-tattooed forearm.

'Nice,' Matt murmured. He swabbed at a vein the size of a small hosepipe and then turned to take the cannula Tori was holding out. 'OK, Snapper. Sharp scratch here. Try and hold still.' The touch of the needle piercing skin was enough to galvanise Snapper, however, and he certainly didn't try to hold still. The smaller men anchoring his arm seemed to just flop clear and the arm came skywards at a speed that sent Matt sprawling backwards to land on top of Tori.

Right on top of her, in fact, in an almost picture-perfect missionary position. One of the burgeoning audience of dry-dock workers hooted with approval.

'Don't mind us, mate,' he yelled. 'You two go right ahead!'

Matt was looking flushed with more than annoyance as he scrambled to a more dignified position.

'Intramuscular midazolam,' he decided. 'Seven point five milligrams.' He gave Tori a grim smile. 'And I know exactly where this needle is going to go.'

Snapper's impressively large buttock made a much easier target than a vein, and the dose of sedative was administered so quickly Matt had time to move well away from the attempted retaliation. The dire threats of what Snapper intended to do to anyone who so much as laid a hand on him became gradually less coherent, and the men assisting with restraint finally breathed a collective sigh of relief.

'Let's get that oxygen on and see what his saturation levels are like,' Matt directed.

John slipped the mask into place and Tori uncurled

the probe in the pocket of the life pack and clipped it onto a sausage-like finger.

'Don't worry, Snapper, this isn't going to hurt. You're doing well.'

Joe was working on the other arm. 'I'm glad we're carrying the oversized cuff,' he remarked. 'We'll still be lucky if the Velcro holds. Blood pressure's 105 on 70,' he reported seconds later.

'What do you want done next, Tori?'

She knew that Matt was testing to see how she would have managed the case if she had still been the most highly qualified person present, and the opportunity was welcome.

'We still need IV access,' she decided aloud. 'We should be targeting a systolic blood pressure of 120 with a head injury, to avoid any secondary insults to the brain from hypoxia and hypotension.' She turned to the monitor. 'Oxygen saturation is 94 per cent. Can you change that acute mask to a high-concentration one, please, John? And make sure the flow is up to 15 litres.'

'Anything else?'

'We might need the fire service to help with extrication.'

'On its way.' Matt nodded. 'I called them as soon as I was shown the top of that ladder.'

'Let's get on with a full secondary survey, then.' Tori reached for the cervical collar that had been abandoned earlier. 'And we're going to need a dressing to cover that head wound.'

It wasn't until Snapper was strapped firmly to a basket-type stretcher, his head well padded and bandaged, IV fluids running and vital signs considered stable, that the ambulance crews were able to stand back temporarily as dock workers and fire service personnel took over shifting the victim from the bottom of the dock to the waiting ambulance far above them at ground level.

Tori stood close to Matt. Maybe a little too close, judging from the grin and the very obvious nod and wink one of Snapper's mates sent in her direction. She didn't embrace a professional response of creating any more distance, however. The reminder of just how Matt had landed on top of her body when he'd been knocked over made her grin right back.

It was only now that she could allow herself any enjoyment of the accidental physical contact and she was not about to deny any pleasure she could get out of it. It was pretty much the *only* physical contact she had had with Matt recently, thanks to the various complications in their home lives that had conspired to keep them apart. It made this morning's little 'accident' rather ironic, Tori decided. Then she changed her mind. Frustrating was a bit more like it.

Taking her gaze off the stretcher being slowly winched up beside the ladder, with firemen holding each end as they climbed, Tori tilted her head to look up at the man standing so close to her. Was Matt missing her as much as she was missing him? Was she the first thing he thought of each morning when he woke and the last thing he thought of at night? And did the thoughts in that private space between waking and sleeping run to the kind of fantasies Tori had never realised she was so good at creating?

As though he felt the sudden heat in her gaze, Matt looked down. Professional detachment lasted only for a heartbeat and the warmth in those hazel eyes let Tori know that Matt knew exactly what she was thinking about. She also had the distinct impression that Matt was just as capable of creating satisfying fantasies as she was.

Matt cleared his throat. 'Hope I didn't hurt you when I fell on top of you like that.'

'Hardly. I'm not a human cushion for nothing.' Tori glanced down at the generous curves covered by her uniform shirt. 'I knew there was a good reason for growing these.'

Joe's chuckle was appreciative, but Matt's line of vision had followed hers and he made an odd kind of sound that might have been a well-stifled groan. Fortunately, it had been covered to any but Tori's ears by Joe's mirth, and Matt looked away instantly.

'They're doing well, aren't they? We're going to have to climb those ladders ourselves in a few minutes.'

To outward appearances, Matt was once again absorbed in watching the stage of the rescue they were not required to assist with, but Tori could feel the tension and it made her smile inwardly. So Matt was just as frustrated as she was, was he?

Time they did something about it, then.

It should have been easy to catch each other for long enough to arrange something and, indeed, their paths crossed quite often enough for the rest of the day, but there always seemed to be others around and conversation had to be general. Even innocuous-seeming feelers about how available they each were became progressively less satisfactory as their shifts wore on.

Matt walked past the back of Tori's ambulance when she was changing an oxygen cylinder, having delivered a patient having a moderate asthma attack.

'How's your dad?' she called.

Matt let go of his end of the stretcher and paused. 'On the mend, finally, thank goodness. He's still coughing, though, and Mum's worried about him, of course.'

Tori smiled. 'I'm pleased to hear that he's getting better.'

'You and me both.' Matt smiled back as his pager sounded. 'Catch you later.'

'Hope so.'

Tori was still smiling. The news that Bob was on the mend was great. The nasty flu Matt's father had contracted three weeks ago, shortly after Matt had fixed her roof, had turned into pneumonia and played havoc with Matt's support system for childcare. The children couldn't stay at their grandparents' house and Linda had been reluctant to leave Bob alone in order to baby-sit for well over a week.

Matt had had to take sick leave himself in order to cover his night duties, and Hayley had apparently been unimpressed with having to care for her siblings before and after school on day-shift days. The stress levels in the two Buchanan households had been far too high to allow Matt any time to himself, but Tori's offer of help had been brushed aside.

'Good grief,' Matt had said. 'The last thing you'd want is a bunch of grumpy kids on your hands. Thanks anyway, Tori, but we'll manage. I'll get a night off next week, I promise.'

Tori's pager sounded as she slotted the oxygen cylinder back into its holder on the floor near the back door of the ambulance. John finished stuffing a pillow into a clean case and dropped it onto the end of the stretcher.

'Casebrook Road. Isn't that where Matt and Joe headed off to?'

The radio crackled to warn of an incoming message. 'Control to Auckland 7.'

Tori reached for the microphone as John slid into the driver's seat. 'Auckland 7 receiving.'

'Priority-one response. You're backing up Auckland 1 at a code 400.'

'Roger.' Tori fastened her seat belt as John flicked on the beacons.

A code 400 was a motor vehicle accident. Tori fished behind her seat to find the fluorescent safety vest needed when working in traffic. Then she pulled a pair of gloves from the box on the console.

'Do you want me to look up Casebrook Road on the map?' she asked John.

'Nah, I'm good. You put your feet up and enjoy the ride.'

Tori grinned. 'I'll do that.'

She would, too. This was great. She was heading in the right direction to see Matt again. The adrenaline-pumping urgency the wail of the siren was advertising had a distinctly personal element in there somewhere.

Matt had never managed that promised night off that week. Tori had been highly suspicious that Hayley's motives in demanding an evening of her uncle's attention had had little to do with an urgent need for tuition before an upcoming maths assessment at school, but if it hadn't, it had been a clever move on the teenager's part.

'It's the first time she's shown any interest in doing well at school,' Matt had explained apologetically when he'd cancelled the planned evening with Tori. 'If

I don't encourage her, I might well kick myself later on.'

Tori could have kicked him right then. The night they had planned to spend together had been the day before Sarah, Ben and Phoebe had arrived back in New Zealand. The visit had only been intended for a day or two to recover from jet-lag before moving into their new house, but there had been a major glitch somewhere on the docks and the container-load of their furniture and personal effects had still not been delivered ten days later.

Not that Tori resented her house guests. Far from it. She was delighted to be reunited with Sarah, and having Phoebe in the house was a joy. Funny how much lonelier and emptier the place had seemed after just that one day when Matt had brought his whole family to help fix the roof.

There was no reason why Matt couldn't visit while the Dawsons were staying, of course, and he had, in fact, spent an evening with them last week. A very enjoyable evening, but Tori could hardly have dragged him away from Ben's animated conversation and whisked him up to her bedroom, could she?

They were getting closer to Casebrook Road now. Tori craned her neck to make sure there was no traffic coming up on the inside lane through the intersection where they were going against a red light.

'Clear this way,' she told John.

'Cool.' John turned off the siren after he turned off the main road. The flashing beacons of the other ambulance could be seen at the end of the road. Matt's ambulance. Tori took a deep, steadying breath.

This was all rather ridiculous. She was twenty-five years old and a free agent. She should be out having fun so why on earth was she pining after a man who had family obligations heavy enough to make it feel like she was waiting to pick up crumbs? She was getting excited over the mere prospect of *seeing* him, for heaven's sake!

Why did she feel as if she was an 'other woman', having an affair with someone who was morally and often physically unavailable?

It *shouldn't* feel like this. They were friends, that's all. The bonus of the best physical relationship she'd ever had was simply that—a bonus. She had absolutely no right to feel frustrated or even resentful. The answer was staring her in the face, of course, but it wasn't until they actually pulled to a stop at the scene on Casebrook Road that it became blindingly unavoidable.

The traffic accident did not appear major. The two cars involved were not badly damaged but there were enough people involved for a second ambulance to have been automatically dispatched as back-up. A police officer was talking to an elderly woman still sitting in her car. Joe was in the back of his ambulance with two people sitting side by side on a stretcher. Matt was outside, crouching in front of a crying child.

He fastened a bandage in place on the small boy's arm and Tori saw him smile and reach out to ruffle the child's thatch of startlingly red hair. A gentle, comforting touch that actually elicited a watery smile on a small and very freckled face.

And Tori felt her own heart squeeze painfully in response to that wobbly smile. Knowing how the touch from Matt's hand would have felt. Loving him for offering that comfort and genuine concern.

Just…loving him.

It took a hard swallow and determined action to open

the door and get moving to shake off the paralysing significance of that moment. Falling in love with Matt Buchanan had never been on Tori's agenda. *She* wasn't the one who was supposed to have been risking heartbreak by allowing the 'extras' into their friendship. *She* had been the one who had made the boundaries so very clear. There had been no point at all in falling in love with Matt so she had been perfectly confident it couldn't possibly happen.

How *could* she have been so incredibly naïve?

Matt had caught a glimpse of that halo of wild blonde curls in the passenger seat of the approaching back-up vehicle. His smile at the child in front of him was an attempt to refocus.

'There you go, tiger.' He ruffled the thick, ginger mop of hair. 'Why don't you jump into the back of the ambulance here and see how Mum's getting on?'

A nod from Joe let Matt know that all was under control inside. The boy's mother and his aunt were shaken up and had some minor cuts and bruises, but there was nothing serious. The elderly female driver from the other vehicle had brushed off any need for assessment, but Matt's instinct was issuing a warning. He moved towards where the woman was still sitting in her car, giving details to a police officer. This time he was going to heed that whisper of instinct.

His direction took him away from where Tori was heading to talk to Joe, but that was probably a good thing right now. The distraction her presence provided was increasing steadily. Why hadn't he heeded the warning that quiet voice in his head had provided in the past? Except he had, hadn't he?

He had known right from the start that this could

happen. Right from that very first conversation with Tori in the staffroom when he had registered that flash of disappointment. It had been laid out on the table in plenty of time for him to avoid repercussions. Victoria Preston would run a mile from raising someone else's children. It didn't matter how incredibly well they got on with each other or how mind-blowingly good the sex might be—there was simply no future in it.

He *accepted* that, dammit! He was happy to take what he could get. Moments of personal joy that brightened his life with enough wattage for the glow to illuminate the darker times. Seeing Tori at work like this was better than nothing, of course, but it wasn't enough.

It could never be *enough*.

'How are you feeling now, Mrs Sanderson?' Matt smiled at the nervous-looking woman as the police officer folded his notebook.

'I'm perfectly fine,' she told him.

'I'd like to check you out anyway, if that's OK.'

'There's absolutely no need. I really can't understand what happened here, but I'm sure it wasn't my fault. I saw the stop sign. I can't possibly have gone through it. I don't *do* things like that. I'm a...a very good driver.'

The police officer gave Matt a meaningful glance as the woman dissolved into sobs and covered her face with her hands.

'We'll be in touch, Mrs Sanderson,' the officer said blandly. 'And the tow truck will take care of your car. They'll be in touch as well.' He moved away, shaking his head. There were plenty of witnesses to confirm the fact that this driver had simply sailed through the stop sign without slackening her speed.

Matt had ignored the glance and the innuendo of the head shake. He took hold of Mrs Sanderson's wrist, noting a rapid and rather thready pulse.

'It's all right,' he said soothingly. 'It's not a nice thing to happen, is it? Gives you a terrible fright.'

Faded blue eyes appeared with an expression of relief. 'But it wasn't my fault.'

'That really doesn't matter right now.' Matt kept up a gentle tone. 'I just want to make sure that you're OK. Getting a fright can make you feel awful, can't it?'

'I do feel a bit shaky,' the woman admitted.

'Are you short of breath at all?'

'Just a little bit.'

'Any chest pain or tightness?'

'Maybe a little.'

'Any dizziness?'

Her voice dropped to a whisper. 'I...I don't feel quite *right*, dear. I'm not sure why, though.'

'Let's see if I can find out. I'm going to take your blood pressure and listen to your chest.' Matt pulled the cuff and stethoscope from his kit. 'Do you have any medical conditions I should know about?'

'I've got high blood pressure,' Mrs Sanderson told him. 'And I do get a bit of angina.'

'Do you use spray for that?'

'Yes.'

'Do you feel like you need to use it now?'

The hesitation was noticeable. 'Would that be all right?'

'Of course it would.' Matt released the valve on the cuff. Two-ten over 145. Mrs Sanderson's blood pressure was not under good control. It was quite high enough to suggest the possibility that something like a transitory ischaemic attack could have blinded her to the stop sign. Especially when a history of angina pointed to existing vessel disease. Either way, using her GTN spray to lower her blood pressure was a good idea.

'I've got my spray right here,' he told her. 'You just lift your tongue and I'll do it for you.'

Tori and John had loaded the other patients into their ambulance for transport to the hospital. Matt managed to ignore the faint wave of desolation as he saw them drive off, because he was focused on persuading Mrs Sanderson that she really needed to go to hospital for a more thorough assessment. Thankfully, due to the level of trust he had already established, and the fact that he refused to discuss any blame regarding the accident, this was not as difficult a task as he had feared. Within ten minutes they had the elderly woman tucked up on a stretcher, receiving some oxygen and having both her heart rhythm and blood pressure monitored carefully as they made their way back towards the Royal.

Matt chose to drive but regretted it. Knowing that Tori would probably still be at the emergency department, handing over all their patients, was more likely to distract him from negotiating the traffic than the other way round.

Life would have been a lot simpler if he hadn't met her again. If he'd stayed on that desk job and let his life revolve purely around the routines and needs of the children. He might have lost a lot of his own identity that way but he was going to lose it anyway, wasn't he? Because Tori made the picture complete.

Made *him* complete.

Imagining life without the friendship they had was

terrifying. Life completely without Tori was unimaginable.

The beep from a car horn behind them made Matt realise the light had changed to green and he hadn't even noticed. This was getting worse. He was getting far too much time for such imaginings, that was the real problem. The last few weeks had been an exercise in frustration, trying to find time together.

Her ambulance *was* still parked in the bay, but Matt released his breath in a long sigh as he slotted his vehicle in beside it. Maybe seeing her at work like this wasn't better than nothing. Every quick smile, every sparkle from those blue eyes…just a glimpse of her in the distance was enough to quicken his pulse. To twist the knot in his gut a little tighter and add to the despair gathering over his life like a black cloud.

And what malevolent god could have orchestrated that little episode this morning? To have fallen on top of Tori like that and get such a searing reminder of what was missing from his life right now was just too much. Keeping the fact that they were lovers so private was a mistake. Matt swung himself purposefully from the driver's seat of the ambulance. It didn't matter who was hanging around. He was going to find some way to arrange some time alone with Tori before he went home today.

They met on station within a few minutes of their shifts finishing.

'Did you call your mother?'

Matt nodded. His smile was somewhat guilty. 'She's happy to stay for a couple of hours. I didn't tell her why, though. I think she assumed I've got a late job or some paperwork to catch up on.'

'I didn't tell Sarah why I'd be late either. She said they'd save the champagne until I got home.'

'Did Ben get that orthopaedic consultancy confirmed, then?'

Tori nodded happily. 'At the Royal, no less. As close to home as it could be. Isn't that great?'

Matt held the door open for Tori and leaned close enough to brush her hair with his lips as she passed. 'The only thing that's better than that,' he whispered, 'is that I'm finally going to get a couple of hours alone with you.'

Tori was biting her lip as they entered the car park. 'But where can we go?' The glint in her eyes was pure mischief. 'I don't suppose you fancy a coffee?'

Matt snorted. 'No. Coffee is *not* what I'm fancying right now.'

Their gazes were still locked when Joe walked past.

'Whoa! This looks serious. Something I should know about here?'

Matt just grinned. 'I should be so lucky.'

Joe shook his head. 'Yeah, you should, mate. 'Bout time you guys came out of the closet if you ask me.'

Tori took a deep breath. 'Did you tell Joe?' she asked. 'About us?'

Matt shook his head. 'All I've ever said to anyone was that we're good friends.'

'Me, too.'

'Maybe I've been giving off vibes. I've…missed you, babe.'

It was hard to get the words past the lump in Tori's throat. 'Me, too.'

'We've got two hours.'

'We can't go home to my place. It would take too long and Sarah and Ben and Phoebe are there.'

'My place is even more crowded than that.' Matt's smile was rueful. 'What shall we do? Go and park up at the beach?'

'For a teenage-style snog?' Tori was grinning. Then her smile faded. 'This is driving me nuts, Matt.'

'Right.' Matt opened his car door. 'Hop in.'

'Where are we going?'

'You'll see.'

Tori's jaw dropped open a few minutes later when Matt pulled his car to a halt. Then she giggled. 'You're *kidding*!'

'I'm perfectly serious.'

'A *motel*?'

'Can you think of anywhere else we're going to get some private time right now?'

'But we're in uniform.'

'I've got some of the kids' jackets in the back. Hayley's will fit you if you want to hide. It's nobody's business but ours anyway. It's not as if we're doing anything *wrong*.'

It seemed like they had never done anything so *right*.

The motel room lacked any of the personality of Tori's bedroom, but after an abstinence of nearly three weeks, neither of them were aware of anything but each other.

It took only seconds to draw the curtains and lock the door and then they were in each other's arms, drowning in a kiss that left them breathless enough to fall onto the huge bed. It was too hard to undress each other lying down, however, and Matt pulled Tori to her feet to grapple with buttons and belts and shoelaces. A desperate need for speed led to clumsiness that made them both laugh, but then their gazes locked and any amusement faded.

The sense of urgency suddenly faded as well. Matt's shirt was only half-unbuttoned and Tori was standing in her bra with her uniform pants still caught halfway down her hips, but nothing existed except that look in Matt's eyes. There was more than a burning desire for her body. The underlying depth of feeling struck a chord that Tori knew mirrored what was feeding her own fierce longing.

She reached up, touching his face softly enough to convey how precious he was to her. She knew she had tears in her eyes but they were tears of joy. Matt *loved* her—just as much as she loved him. For now—for the next two hours, in fact—that was all that mattered.

His kiss was as gentle as her touch on his face had been. And now his hands were moving slowly. The fastening on her bra came undone, the straps slipped free from her arms and Tori revelled in the exquisite pain as her nipples tightened even further under the brush of those slow, sure hands. Her own hands were still raised, her fingers tracing the outlines of his face, touching his lips and even his tongue between kisses.

They already knew each other so well, but this was the first time they had made love since Tori had recognised how she felt about Matt. The first time she had realised that the overwhelming emotional bond was reciprocated. They were lovers in far more than a physical sense, and what happened between them now was far more profound than Tori had ever imagined lovemaking could be.

It went way beyond fun. Way beyond satisfaction. It was dangerously close to being a vital part of her existence. A part of her soul she would not survive without.

In the quiet circle of Matt's arms when passion had been, at least, temporarily sated, Tori found the courage to say it.

'I think I'm addicted to you, Matt Buchanan. I can't survive without this.'

His arms tightened. 'Tell me about it, babe. I've been going slowly mad over the last three weeks.'

'This is so crazy. We're in a motel, for heaven's sake! Like we're having an affair or something.'

'When that furniture turns up, we'll be able to get back to normal. I can come and visit you.'

'But it's still weird, isn't it? We snatch bits of time together here and there and make sure nobody knows we're anything more than good friends.'

'Are we, Tori?' Matt's voice was very soft. 'Are we more than good friends?'

'If we were just good friends, it wouldn't matter that our lives were so complicated or that we only got to see each other when there were other people around, would it? If we were doing this just for fun, we'd enjoy it when it happened and wouldn't worry about it if it didn't.'

'I did warn you.' Matt's voice tickled Tori's ear. 'I knew it was quite likely I'd fall in love with you.'

'But I didn't think I'd fall in love with you.' Tori twisted in Matt's arms so she could see his face properly. Could touch it again. 'This is a disaster, Matt.'

But Matt's expression looked anything but dismayed. 'Are you saying you're in love with me?' He seemed to get the answer he wanted from her touch and turned his head to press a kiss into her palm. 'Oh…*Tori*. Sweetheart, I'm sorry.'

'Why are you sorry?'

'Well, I'm not, of course. Not for me. You've got no idea how happy it makes me. I'm sorry for you. I didn't want you to end up getting hurt.'

'Maybe I won't. Maybe we can still make it work.'

Matt went very still. 'How?'

'I think Joe's right. We should come out of the closet. We should let people know how we feel about each other and spend more time together. Then it won't matter if we're not always alone. It won't even matter if we've got our whole families around.'

'Won't it? The kids would drive you nuts, wouldn't they?'

'I'm not planning to live with you, Matt. I liked having them around that day you came to fix the roof. I'd rather spend time with you like that than not see you.'

'But Hayley might give you a hard time. It might be enough to put you off me completely.'

'You might go off me when you've spent enough time in my company.'

'Doubt it.' Matt pressed another kiss onto Tori's face. And another. 'I could never go off you, babe.'

'We may as well find out. Let's do it.'

'Out of the closet?'

'Yeah.'

'This isn't a kill-it-or-cure-it scenario, is it?'

Tori laughed. 'I hope not.'

'I'm still not sure. I don't want the kids chasing you into the distance. You're too important to me, Tori.'

'I'm tougher than I look, Matt. I can take whatever Hayley wants to dish out. She might not even be that bothered, you know.' Tori was still smiling happily. 'I mean, it's not as if I'm intending to *marry* you or anything, is it?'

CHAPTER EIGHT

'ARE you going to marry Uncle Matt?'

'Just because grown-ups are special friends, it doesn't mean they have to get married, Bonnie.'

'But you're his girlfriend, aren't you, Tori?'

'Yes, Jack.' Tori couldn't resist smiling at the deceptively angelic face turned up to her as she sat between the twins on the front steps of Matt's house. 'Is that cool?'

'Yeah…' Jack's eyebrows disappeared under the blond curls. 'Does that mean we get to play at *your* house sometimes?'

'Of course.'

'And go swimming at the beach?'

'Sure.'

'Do we get to sleep over at your house?'

'Maybe.' Tori was less sure of her ground here. 'You'd better ask Uncle Matt about that.'

'But you've got *lots* of beds.'

'That's true. But I've got visitors at the moment.'

'Who?'

'My sister, Sarah, and her husband, Ben, and their little girl, Phoebe. And Sarah's going to have a baby soon.'

'Are you going to have a baby soon, too, Tori?'

'*Bonnie!*' The voice from the doorway behind them was horrified. 'You can't ask questions like that!'

'But I want to know,' Bonnie protested. '*Are* you, Tori?'

'No, chicken. I'm just planning to enjoy Sarah's baby. I'll be an aunty for the first time.'

'If you married Uncle Matt, you could be *our* aunty,' Jack informed her with the air of imparting a great truth.

'That's true.' Laughing, Tori stood up. 'Do you want some help with dinner, Matt?' *Please* say you want some help with dinner was the message she tried to send telepathically.

Matt grinned. 'Sure. And you two can go and get on with your homework. No TV until I've heard your reading and tested those spelling words and times tables.'

'Oh, but—'

'No "buts",' Matt said firmly. 'And, no, Tori is not going to help tonight. She has to come into the kitchen and help me with dinner.' He lowered his voice. 'And have a glass of wine.'

'You're a hero, Matt. I was losing the battle out there.' But Tori was still smiling as she watched the twins reluctantly retrieve their school backpacks from the end of the hallway. 'They're neat kids, aren't they?'

'They always have been.' Matt nodded. His fond smile faded, however, as the sound of voices raised in anger emanated from the living room. The twins looked up anxiously but Matt was reassuring. 'It's OK, guys, I'll sort it. You take your homework into the kitchen.'

Tori followed him as he strode towards the source of the friction. Hayley had her arms folded and her nose in the air. Charles was clutching a somewhat crumpled shoebox and looked to be on the verge of tears.

'What's going on?' Matt queried.

'She *broke* it!' Charles accused loudly.

Hayley's sigh was long suffering. 'It was, like…an *accident*?'

'It was *not*!'

'You left it lying in the middle of the freakin' floor, you idiot!'

'I did *not*! You stood on it. On *purpose*!'

'OK, that's enough.' Matt stepped between the two children and Tori saw his brow crease in concern as he glanced down at Charles. For someone who was so reserved, it had to be a fairly catastrophic disaster to have him this publicly upset. Matt's tone gentled. 'What's broken, mate?'

'My…my…'

'His stupid, *disgusting* rat's skeleton,' Hayley supplied.

'I…I was going to take it to school tomorrow. For my science project.'

'*Eeeww!* As if anyone wants to see *that*!'

'Hayley, I told you, that's enough.' Matt hadn't raised his voice but Tori thought it would take a very brave person to ignore the warning in his tone. 'I'd like you to apologise to Charles and then go to your room.'

Hayley opened her mouth, clearly ready to defy Matt, but then her gaze flicked towards Tori. Her mouth snapped shut and she jerked her head dismissively.

'Oh, *whatever*!' she snapped. Seconds later, the door slammed behind her.

Tori found Charles looking at her as well, but his gaze slid away without registering a response to her sympathetic smile.

'I'm sorry, mate,' Matt told him. 'Whether or not it was deliberate, it was a rotten thing to happen.'

'It's Hayley that's rotten. I hate her.'

'Life's not that easy for Hayley right now. She'll be a lot nicer to have around again one of these days.'

'When?'

'Maybe when she turns eighteen.' Matt gave Charles's shoulder a soft punch. 'Do you reckon we can hold out till then, buddy? With a bit of male solidarity?'

Tori found herself smiling again as she saw the shy glance of hero-worship from the bespectacled twelve-year-old.

'I reckon.'

'Now, about that science project.' Matt peered inside the shoebox and clicked his tongue sadly. Then his tone became very thoughtful. 'You might not know this, Charles, but somewhere in all those boxes out in the garage is a human skeleton that your dad bought when he was at medical school.'

Charles's eyes widened dramatically. 'A *real* one?'

'No, I think it's plastic,' Matt said. 'But it *looks* real and it's lifesize. It's got a stand, I seem to remember, and there's a hook in the skull so it hangs.' Matt grinned at Tori. 'He was a huge hit at parties, I believe. Went by the name of Jonesy.' He turned back to Charles. 'How would it be if we go and dig out that box after dinner and you take Jonesy to school for your project?'

Charles stirred the contents of the shoebox with his hand. 'But I really liked *my* skeleton.'

'You can come and have another poke around the stables at the weekend, if you like,' Tori offered. 'Maybe you can find another one. When's the science project due?'

'Next week.'

'There you go, then. How 'bout Uncle Matt brings you up on Saturday?'

'I've got a day shift on Saturday, remember?'

'Oh.' Tori smiled at Charles. 'I could come and get you if you like.'

There was a flash of something like interest, but then Charles kicked at a piece of carpet with his toe. 'I dunno,' he muttered. He peeped up at Matt. 'Can I see Jonesy first?'

Hayley sulked throughout the evening meal a short time later, picking at her food and scowling when anyone said anything to her.

'Did you know it takes twice as many muscles to frown as it does to smile?' Matt asked no one in particular.

'Does it?' Tori wasn't sure whether that was correct, but what did it matter? 'I'll have to remember that when I'm trying to burn off extra calories.'

Hayley glared at her. 'Are you saying I'm *fat*?'

'Hardly. I wish I looked half as good in jeans as you do.'

'You look *nice* in jeans, Tori,' Bonnie said stoutly.

'Yeah.' The wiggle of Matt's eyebrows was suggestive. Charles reddened slightly. The twins giggled. Hayley pushed back her chair and stood up abruptly.

'Oh, pul-*lease*!'

'Sit down, Hayley. You haven't finished your meal.'

'I've had enough.' The glance towards Tori was pointed. 'I've got homework to do.' Her tone was more than faintly sarcastic. 'May I, please, be excused, Uncle Matt?'

'Sure.' He seemed to ignore her flouncing from the

room without missing a beat. In fact, he smiled at the twins. 'Any good stuff happen at school today, kids?'

The twins' cheerful response was enough to dust any lingering antipathy from Hayley's company under the proverbial carpet, and they kept it up as they helped Tori do the dishes after dinner, while Matt and Charles went foraging amongst the boxes in the garage. It dimmed noticeably, however, when their uncle returned and informed them it was time for bed.

'But we're not tired, Uncle Matt.'

'It's 7.30,' he said firmly. 'And you know what that means.' He advanced on the children, who shrieked in glee, clearly anticipating a customary game.

Tori was laughing as hard as the twins by the time he had chased, cornered, pounced and caught two very determined seven-year-olds. They dangled, one under each arm, still giggling between protests as they were carted off towards their bedroom.

Charles followed half an hour later but Hayley insisted on watching a favourite television programme that didn't finish until 9.45 p.m.

'It was a small victory for her,' Matt explained, when he and Tori were finally alone in the living room, curled up on the couch together. 'What she didn't know was that, besides finishing her homework, Charles told me she *had* apologised to him when we weren't around to hear.'

Tori snuggled a bit closer. 'You're great with those kids, Matt.'

'I just do my best.'

'But you manage so well. I wouldn't know where to start in handling Hayley. You seem to know when to back off. If you'd forced her to apologise, it wouldn't have meant much to either her or Charles, would it?'

'I think you just need to pick your battles when it comes to teenagers,' Matt responded. 'Doesn't mean I'm a soft touch, though. I've got my bottom lines and they know they have boundaries they can't cross. You were right about those boundaries being important. Like a safety net, I guess. Makes them feel secure if they can push them but can't get past them.'

Was there a hidden meaning to Matt's words? A reference to *her* bottom line about their relationship? Was he trying to make her feel secure by not crossing it? By reprimanding the children for questions relating to a shared future? Tori didn't want to think about it. She couldn't imagine a future without this man beside her, and it was far too soon to start letting her enjoyment of being with him and the children erode a long-held vow. You could worry too much about the future anyway, and it could lessen your enjoyment of the present.

This time alone with Matt was way too precious to waste. She rested her head on his shoulder. 'I get to see a whole new side of you when the kids are around.'

'The stupid side, you mean?' Matt's arm enclosed Tori in a circle that closed any potential gap between them. 'Like wrestling seven-year-olds?'

Tori's face tilted upwards. 'You're pretty good at wrestling.' She licked her lips and Matt's eyes darkened instantly.

'You wanna wrestle, babe?'

'Mmm.'

The kiss was none the less welcome for being expected. In fact, having to wait for it until the children were all in bed made it all the more exciting. It was just a pity they couldn't go to bed themselves, but that would hardly be fair on the kids. Tori couldn't afford to become an integral part of their lives yet. What if they ended up being casualties in the long term?

The conversation with the twins on the step today was a bit of a worry really. It was only two weeks since she and Matt had 'come out of the closet', but the youngest children weren't the only ones hinting at expectations of a permanent future for the couple.

Linda's embrace when Tori had joined the extended family for a meal last week had been as welcoming as her own mother's might have been, and Sarah had had an irritatingly knowing smile on her face on several occasions over the last few days. It was there again when Tori finally arrived home late that night.

'You're in love with him,' she informed Tori with satisfaction, after hearing about her evening.

'I told *you* that.'

'No, but you're *really* in love with him. You won't give up, kids or no kids.' Sarah waved a hand happily. 'It's about time this house was full of children again. Carol would be thrilled.'

'That isn't going to happen,' Tori insisted. Was that sudden chill down her spine a touch of panic, perhaps? 'This isn't just *my* house, anyway. Remember?'

'It is as far as I'm concerned,' Sarah said. 'Ben and I have our own place now. Our furniture's definitely being delivered tomorrow, by the way, so we should be out of here by Wednesday.'

Tori tried to look as delighted as Sarah but failed. 'I'm going to miss having you around, Sas.'

'We're only just down the road. Besides, there are good reasons why you don't want us hanging around. You want to bring Matt home sometimes, don't you? *Without* Ben monopolising his company?'

Tori grinned. 'There is that, I suppose.'

'It would be a lot simpler if the kids stayed as well.'

'Matt's mother's offered to stay over with them so we can get a whole night to ourselves sometimes.'

'That's nice of her.'

'Yeah. It should work brilliantly.'

It did work brilliantly for all of two weeks.

On the night they chose to spend together during the third week, Matt's cellphone rang at 10 p.m. Lying so close to him in bed after their love-making, Tori was able to hear quite clearly how upset Linda sounded on the other end of the line.

'Hayley's missing.'

'What? It's ten o'clock at night!'

'I know. I just went in to check on the twins and I noticed her door was open. She's not in bed. She's not in the house, Matt, and I don't know what to do.'

'Have you tried calling her cellphone?'

'I just get her voicemail. I've left messages.'

'I'm on my way.' Matt swung his legs out of bed and Tori couldn't hear Linda any more. 'No,' Matt said firmly a few seconds later. 'Don't wake Dad, and of course you need to stay where you are with the other children. I'll be there in twenty minutes. Call me if she turns up in the meantime.'

Tori scrambled out of bed as well. 'I'm coming, too.'

'Are you sure you want to?'

'Do *you* want me to? I'll stay out of it if you think it's better. I mean, it's obvious that Hayley's doing this because she knows I'm with you. That makes me the problem here, doesn't it?'

Matt's fingers stilled for a moment as he buttoned his shirt. 'I think we might have reached one of those bottom lines here. Hayley is going to have to realise that I'm not about to let her manipulate me into staying away from you, in which case it's going to make a statement if you're with me.' His smile was both apologetic and a little wistful. 'Besides, I think I could do with the back-up.'

'You've got it.' Tori hauled on her jeans and reached for her shoes. 'I hope she's OK. She's only fifteen, after all. Where on earth would she have gone?'

'She'll be with one of her mates, I expect. She'll probably have turned up by the time we get home, and if it wasn't for the fact that Mum's so upset I might well have left it for a while longer.' Matt shook his head grimly as he blew out the last candle. 'I intend to have words with that young lady when we find her.'

'I couldn't sleep. I went for a walk. What's the big deal?'

'The big deal, Hayley, is that you are fifteen years old. You do not leave this house at night without permission.'

'I'm nearly sixteen. You're not my father. You can't tell me what to do.'

Matt simply stared at her. It was Hayley that dropped her gaze.

'Do you have any idea how worried Nanna was?'

'I can look after myself.'

'You've just given a very good demonstration of how irresponsible you're capable of being. You were sitting on a park bench when we finally found you, for God's sake, Hayley. At eleven o'clock at night. By yourself. Have you really got no idea how *dangerous* that is?'

Hayley's dismissive snort fell into a charged silence. They were all sitting around the table in Matt's kitchen.

Linda still held a crumpled wad of tissues in her hand and her eyes were red. With a sinking heart Tori realised that it was going to be unfair to expect the children's grandmother to keep up these kind of babysitting duties. She had enough to worry about with Bob's slow recovery from his illness, and she was already doing far more than most grandparents in the way of childcare support. Taking responsibility for Hayley after this would be a frightening prospect.

Matt sat at the other end of the table and Tori was at right angles to him. Close enough to touch, but she was careful not to. It had been dark enough by that park for Hayley not to have seen Tori sitting in the car when Matt had marched over to the bench and ordered her into the vehicle in no uncertain terms. Her expression, when she went to get into the front passenger seat and found it already occupied, had been more than enough to confirm that the attention Tori was claiming from Matt had been the motivation for her bad behaviour.

Was Matt right in thinking that if Hayley knew she wasn't going to win, she would accept the inevitable and change her attitude? Tori wasn't at all sure but, then, hadn't she commended Matt on his ability to handle the teenager? She had no idea of the best way through this. The only thing she was certain of was that she didn't want to lose Matt.

Ever.

Matt glanced at his watch. 'Go to bed, Hayley.'

She stood up slowly, eyes downcast, and her hesitation suggested that she was expecting more in the way of punishment. Matt didn't let her down.

'You're grounded, Hayley. You don't leave this

house for the next week except to go to school. And I'm confiscating your cellphone for the week as well.'

That hurt. Hayley straightened defiantly. 'You can't do that.'

'Just watch me.'

'No!' Hayley almost stamped her foot. 'I won't let you take my phone. You can't do that. You're *not* my father and I don't *have* to do what you say.'

Matt's chair scraped harshly as he pushed it back to stand up and face the teenager.

'No, I'm not your father. I wish he was here. And your mum. And it's very, very sad that they're not here because I know how much they loved you.'

Tori's throat constricted with the prickle of imminent tears as she saw the lines of pain on Matt's face. She had to fight the urge to stand up herself and take him into her arms. Linda made a sniffling sound and reached for a fresh handful of tissues.

'I'm doing my best here, Hayley,' Matt said quietly. 'And I'm doing it because I loved your parents. And I love you.'

Hayley stared at the floor, her shoulders hunched defensively.

'I'm not your father,' Matt repeated. 'But unfortunately I'm the closest thing to him that you and your brothers and sisters have now. I'm going to continue doing my best to take his place because I've made a promise to do that and I don't break my promises.'

Matt took a deep breath. 'I love you, Hayley, but I also love Tori. It's a very different kind of love and having Tori around isn't going to make any difference to the way I love you or the other children. The only difference it could make would be to make me happier, and if she's prepared to put up with you lot and stick around then it's going to make us all happier, believe me.'

Matt was putting a lot on the line here for Tori. Never mind the fact that Linda was nodding approval at the other end of the table. If Hayley chose to be completely alienated by this bottom line, it could affect the relationship Matt had with his nieces and nephews for ever. Matt was clearly prepared to take that risk, however. Because of how much he loved her. Tori swallowed hard to try and clear that constriction in her throat.

'Giving Tori a hard time could drive her away, which is probably what you had in mind,' Matt continued quietly. 'That's something I really, really don't want to happen.'

It was the catch in his voice that was Tori's undoing. He was possibly suffering more than anyone else in this room right now, and she couldn't let that continue.

'It's not *going* to happen, Matt,' she whispered. 'I love you, too, remember?'

Matt's gaze swivelled. 'Enough to put up with my whole family? There's a few more teenagers on the way, you know.'

'More than enough.'

They both looked at Hayley. Was this affirmation enough to make her realise she wasn't going to win? Had Matt's words of love touched her as deeply as they had touched Tori? Her head was bowed and in the silence that followed Tori's words she and Matt looked at each other.

The love in those warm hazel eyes was all that Tori wanted to see. All that she could be aware of. It didn't matter that they weren't alone in the room because the message she was receiving, and hopefully sending, was powerful enough to make them seem alone.

Matt's voice was barely more than a whisper.

'Enough to...to marry me, Tori?'

No. No one else existed in this moment of time. Just the man she loved *so* much. Tori was smiling—and crying, as she spoke.

'More than enough.'

CHAPTER NINE

PERSONALITIES couldn't change with the flick of a switch.

And the kind of turn-around Matt Buchanan's niece was demonstrating would have engendered suspicion in even the most trusting soul.

'Hayley's up to something,' Tori warned Matt. 'I can feel it.'

'She's certainly been behaving extraordinarily well ever since the night we got engaged.' Matt paused and then shook his head. 'But nobody could keep up that much of an act for two straight weeks, surely?'

'Depends on how strong the motivation is.' Tori glanced through the window to where Hayley was sitting on the lawn, her cellphone pressed to her ear. 'I just have this horrible feeling she's trying to lull us into a false sense of security.'

'No.' Matt sounded rather smug. 'She's just come to her senses. She trod on one of those bottom lines and has enough sense to respect it.' He put down the tea-towel he was using to dry dishes and pulled Tori into his arms. 'Are you really worried, hon? Are you regretting your decision to help me take on this tribe?'

Tori accepted his kiss more than willingly. Then she gave him one of her own. 'No way. The more I've thought about it, the more sense it makes. I suspect it's fate. Or genes, maybe. I grew up with a family that wasn't exactly related and I must have learned a bit on the way. I've had my years of freedom and now here

I am in that huge house that's just crying out to be stuffed full of people again. Besides, I love you, in case you hadn't noticed. And part of what I love about you is the way you are with those kids.'

'Kismet,' Matt agreed happily. 'But I don't expect you to be a mother to that lot. I'll take full responsibility for keeping them in line. If Hayley causes trouble again, I'll deal with it, I promise. All I ask is that you give them all a chance.'

'The twins are a breeze,' Tori assured him. 'I love them to bits. And Charles is coming out of his shell with me now. He's a neat kid.'

'You've made him feel special,' Matt smiled. 'Look at him.' He turned, with Tori still in his arms, so they could both see out of the kitchen window.

Charles was sitting under a tree, his face creased with lines of fierce concentration as he studied his finger positions for the guitar chord he was trying to master.

'You couldn't have given him better motivation for throwing himself into those guitar lessons.'

Tori laughed. 'We'd better not set a date for the wedding until he's quite confident of whatever song he chooses to play for us.'

They pulled apart as Hayley entered the room, but she seemed too engrossed in her conversation to notice how close the embrace had been.

'And did you, like, see what she was *wearing*? Who does she think she *is*? Talk about skank!' There was a pause and then Hayley sighed dramatically. 'I have *no* idea... Yeah, I'm allowed to go but I can't go if I've got nothing to wear, can I?'

'I'd better go and get the twins to bed.' Matt left,

and by the time Tori had finished putting the cutlery away, Hayley had finished her conversation.

'What have you got nothing to wear to?' Tori asked casually.

'There's a disco at school on Friday night.'

'What sort of things do they wear to discos these days?'

'Oh, miniskirts or jeans, crop tops. You know.'

'Maybe Matt can take you shopping some time this week.'

'Doubt it.'

'Why not?'

'He's, like, a *guy*?' Hayley's tone suggested that Tori's mental faculties were definitely in question. 'No way am I going to be seen clothes shopping with a *guy*.'

'Right.' Tori smiled, mainly because Hayley's tone was a lot closer to the way she'd previously talked to her. Maybe her suspicions were unfounded. Matt was right, she had to give the teenager a chance. What choice did she have, in fact, when she was planning to spend at least the next few years living in the same house as Hayley?

'I don't s'pose you'd come.'

'Come where? To the disco?'

Hayley looked incredulous for the length of time it took to realise Tori was pulling her leg. Then she shrugged. 'Shopping,' she said succinctly.

'You want me to come clothes shopping with you?' It was hard not to sound as incredulous as Hayley had looked a moment ago.

The teenager shrugged again. 'Sure. Why not?' A rather intent gaze was fixed on Tori. 'I know what shops I want to go to,' she said. 'And I know just what sort of clothes I really need, but they're, like, label stuff, you know? Uncle Matt wouldn't understand. He'd think they were too expensive or something.'

'I'll have a word with him if you like,' Tori offered. 'Make him realise that the *right* clothes can never be too expensive.'

'What's too expensive?' Matt had come back into the kitchen. He raised his eyebrows at Hayley and then caught Tori's expression. 'What? Am I interrupting something here?'

'Girl talk,' Tori informed him. 'Important stuff. As in clothes to wear to the disco on Friday night.'

Matt groaned. 'I don't have to go shopping, do I?'

'Tori said she'd go with me,' Hayley informed him with glib inaccuracy, but Tori didn't bother to correct her.

'I'll make sure we don't buy anything that costs the earth,' she promised Matt.

'You haven't had any new clothes for a while,' Matt responded. He grinned at Tori. 'You girls go out and buy whatever you want. It's on me.'

'Wouldn't you rather go with your friends?' Tori asked Hayley. 'And Matt's credit card?'

'Hang on a minute,' Matt protested. 'I'm not sure I like *that* idea.'

'Me neither,' Hayley said firmly. 'It's *you* I want to go shopping with, Tori. Please?'

How could she resist a chance to actually bond with this, the most difficult member of her soon-to-be adopted family?

'Sure. I'd love to go with you, Hayley. I'm off on Wednesday. Would that suit you?'

Hayley was actually smiling. Tori had never seen her

look so pleased. 'Sweet,' she pronounced. 'Hey, thanks, Tori.'

'My pleasure.'

The pleasure lasted for at least an hour and a half on Wednesday afternoon. It had been a long time since Tori had done the rounds of teenage boutiques in one of the bigger malls, and it was great fun. She even tried on a couple of things herself in between admiring Hayley's choices of garments to try on. The discernment Hayley was showing was commendable as well. There were no impulse decisions and a tour of every available shop was made before starting again to narrow down the choice.

The only minor disagreement was over a pair of designer jeans with a price tag that made Tori laugh.

'Sorry, Hayley, but no way!'

'You said the *right* clothes could never be too expensive.'

'One hundred and fifty dollars for jeans is expensive. Three hundred dollars is a joke.'

'They have a good label,' Hayley sniffed.

'Must be made of pure gold, then. Who, in their right minds, would pay that much for a pair of jeans?'

'People who want to *look* good?' The look Hayley bestowed on Tori was enough to still molten lava.

'Try the other pair on again. I really can't see much difference myself.'

The second pair of jeans was tossed over the curtain of the cubicle a minute later. 'These'll do, I guess.'

Tori picked them up. So much for a bonding experience. She'd had about enough of shopping with Hayley now. 'Are we done, then? You've got those two tops already.'

'Yeah. I guess. Do you want to go and pay for them while I get changed?' Hayley poked her nose through the gap in the curtains. 'Shove the other bags in here and I'll look after them.'

Hayley carried the shopping bags as they made their way from the shop. When they passed the security barriers and the strident beeping signalled a problem, Tori eyed the carrier bags and groaned inwardly. Had Hayley wanted those designer jeans enough to think she could stuff them in with her previous purchases and get away with it? Did she not know about the tags?

The two security officers eyed Hayley suspiciously as well. 'Open your bags,' they ordered her.

Hayley complied instantly. 'It must be a mistake,' she insisted. 'I would *never* shoplift!'

'I have all the receipts for those items,' Tori added. 'Maybe there's an extra tag they forgot to take off.'

The security officers exchanged a glance, having searched the bags Hayley carried.

'Could you open *your* bag, please, ma'am?'

'What?' Tori blinked. 'Oh…*my* bag. Of course. Here.' She pulled open her shoulder-bag and held it out.

The security officers exchanged another glance. 'Could you come with us, please, ma'am?'

'What?' Tori was stunned. 'What for?'

'Store policy,' she was informed. 'Unless you want to talk to the police standing here in the doorway?'

Passing shoppers were staring. Some had stopped in their tracks. Tori, her face flushing furiously to make up for that first reaction of going pale, snatched her bag back and looked inside. She looked up, startled, and caught Hayley's expression for a split second before it was expertly masked. And she understood only too well what had happened here.

'She's not my mother,' Hayley was telling the security officers now. 'Just a friend of my uncle's. And I heard her promise him that she wouldn't *buy* something that cost the earth.'

'I've never been more humiliated in my whole life.'

'What did Matt say when you rang him up to tell him you'd been arrested for shoplifting?'

'He was great, Sas. He arrived there in his uniform, having left work early. He knew one of the police officers, which helped, and I know they believed him when he said it was a set-up by Hayley. But...'

'Don't cry, Tori,' Sarah pleaded. 'You've been so happy—I hate to hear you sounding this upset.'

'But everything's going wrong and it's all my fault.'

'What?'

'There's been this *huge* row. Matt's parents came over and there was a kind of family court thing. Matt said Hayley had gone way too far this time and he'd had more than enough. And...and Hayley was shouting back, saying she didn't want him pretending to be her father and she certainly wasn't going to put up with *me* pretending to be her mother. It was all just awful and I feel like it's my fault because if I wasn't around, she wouldn't be behaving like this.'

'She'd find something else to perform about if it wasn't you,' Sarah said. 'She's a teenager after all.'

Tori was crying again. 'I'm going to have a police record if I'm convicted. I won't be able to get a permanent job as an ambulance officer. I'll probably be fired from being a nurse.' She drew in a shaky breath, trying to compose herself. It failed. 'The other children are so frightened at the trouble Hayley's in. Matt and Linda decided it would be better if she went to stay with her grandparents for a few days until things calm down, and Bonnie was distraught when she saw her packing a bag. Matt's with her now, trying to settle her down.'

'Do you want to come and stay with me? Shall I come and get you?'

'No.' Tori made another effort to pull herself together and this time she was more successful. 'I offered to leave as soon as we got home from the police station but Matt thought it would just convince Hayley that she could win this battle, and his parents agreed. He says we'll get through it but we need to stick together and stay strong.'

'He might be right.' But Sarah didn't sound too sure. 'Let me know if there's anything I can do to help, won't you?'

'I don't think anyone can help just now,' Tori said miserably. 'It's horrible, Sas. Things couldn't be worse.'

Except they could.

Things became much worse the next day when Linda and Bob arrived at Matt's house as they were clearing up after dinner. The twins had raced off to watch TV and Charles was up in his room, practising on his guitar.

Matt looked at his parents' faces as they entered the kitchen. 'Oh, no! What's happened? Is it Hayley?'

Bob nodded heavily. 'You'd better sit down, son. Hayley's run away again.'

'Did you check the park?'

Linda didn't seem to hear Matt. 'She told us she was

going to Gemma's place to do homework after school and she'd catch a bus and be home by dinnertime. That's why we didn't worry until she was late for dinner. She even left us Gemma's address and phone number.'

'So you rang?'

Linda nodded slowly. 'Gemma said Hayley hadn't been at school and they'd never made plans to do any homework. So we checked her room. Her stuff's gone, Matt. And…and she left a note saying not to bother looking for her because this time she's gone for good.'

Matt ran his hand through his hair in an agitated gesture. 'I suppose you've tried her cellphone?'

'She left it behind.' Linda's voice broke. 'On top of the note.'

'Can I see the note?' Matt looked as white as a sheet now and Tori could understand why. The significance of Hayley abandoning her precious cellphone was not lost on any of them. This was deadly serious.

Matt read the note in silence and then handed it to Tori.

You don't have to worry about me any more, it read, *I can look after myself. You don't need me around. You've got Tori. Don't bother looking for me coz you won't find me. I'm never coming back.*

'Oh, my God,' Tori breathed. 'She's done this because of me.'

'It's my fault, not yours,' Matt said heavily. 'I shouldn't have tried to force the issue.'

So she and Matt being together was an 'issue' now. One that shouldn't have been forced. Had they both been so blindly in love they hadn't seen that Hayley's antagonism stemmed from insecurity?

'You don't think she'd…' Linda blew her nose, unable to finish her sentence.

'Hurt herself?' Matt voiced what they were all thinking. 'I don't know,' he said miserably. 'But I really don't think so. This isn't a suicide note. It's a cry for help, isn't it? She thinks she's not wanted. Or that she's too much trouble or something.'

'She knows perfectly well that we'll shift heaven and earth to find her,' Bob said.

'Does she?' Matt sighed. 'I think that's what she's trying to find out. What worries me is how difficult she's going to make this. Just what is it going to take to prove how much we care?'

'I think she's issuing an ultimatum,' Tori said quietly. 'A choice for you, Matt. Either her or me.'

'But that's ridiculous. She can't do that!'

'She sees me as a threat. I'm taking too much of you away from these children, Matt.' She blinked back tears. 'You thought the difficult thing would be to find someone prepared to help you raise this family, but maybe what's going to be impossible is finding someone that the family will accept.'

'But I *need* you,' Matt said desperately. 'We all need you. Hayley just can't see it.'

'And maybe she never will. And she's just proved that it could never work unless she does.' For the first time since Matt had put his foot down about Hayley trying to manipulate his behaviour regarding Tori, she could see a flicker of doubt in his eyes, and that was painful enough to wipe out the anguish of concern for Hayley for just a split second. Then it returned in full force.

'We're wasting time here,' Tori said. 'I can't come and help you search because I'm the last person who should be around if you find her. What I can do, though, is ring around all her schoolfriends. If you give me Gemma's home phone number, I'll start from there.'

'We're going to need to go to the police if we don't find her in the next couple of hours,' Matt said calmly. 'Let's hope they know more than we do about where teenagers can make themselves disappear in this city.'

Unfortunately, the police knew far more than Matt expected. They knew just how hard it was to find a teenager who had decided to make herself vanish, and there were definite limits on how many resources they could spare to help.

An article, with Hayley's photograph, went into the major newspapers the following day. Radio and television news broadcasts ran an appeal for the next two days. The school community was informed and asked to come forward with any information that might help. Hayley's closer friends were all interviewed.

'We're getting the same story,' an officer reported to Matt. 'She wasn't happy with what was happening at home and she had been talking about running away for weeks.'

For weeks. When had that corner been turned? Had it simply been aimed at Tori or had the seeds been sown with the first hint that Matt's attention had not been fully focused on the children? That he wanted just a little time for himself? That first hint of real trouble, when Hayley had been in trouble for swearing at her teacher, had come well before he'd started anything more than a friendship with Tori, hadn't it? He had only been planning to go away for a weekend to attend Sarah's wedding in Fiji.

Had Hayley taken his relationship with Tori as a

personal rejection? Had that night she'd taken herself to the park been some kind of trial run? How much further had she gone this time after the way Matt had laid down the law about not tolerating interference in his relationship with Tori? Matt would never forgive himself if anything had happened to Hayley. Never. No matter how strongly he felt about Tori, he should never have let their relationship interfere with the fragile dynamics of the new family he had created. This was *his* fault.

'She must be somewhere out on the streets.' For the sake of sanity it was essential to try and redirect the anger his own actions had generated, and Matt had only one target available. 'She needs protection, for God's sake. You and I both know what goes on out there. The drug scene—the prostitution to pay for the drugs. Who knows what she's being forced into? We can't just sit back and wait for her to come home any more. What the hell are you guys actually *doing*?'

'Unfortunately, there's not a lot else we *can* do. Not unless we get some more information. We've checked all the usual haunts for street kids and nobody's seen her.'

'So they say!'

'You've advertised widely. I've seen the posters up all over the place.'

Tori had helped him with those posters. They'd given up another useless night of trying to sleep and had driven all over the city, sticking them to lampposts and billboards far and wide.

'Police stations nationwide have been alerted. Everybody's doing their best to help, Matt.'

Nationwide. Yes, Hayley could have left the city.

The thought of her hitchhiking made Matt's blood run cold.

'She won't get out of the country, even if she does have her passport.'

'I just wish I'd given her a credit card now. At least we'd know whether she was still in the city or not.'

'In some ways, no news is good news,' the officer reminded Matt quietly. 'Hang in there, mate. She may well turn up none the worse for a few days living rough.'

They were all exhausted by the third day of searching. The atmosphere in the Buchanan household was grim. Bonnie was constantly in tears. Charles had withdrawn to a silent ghost-like state and even sunny little Jack was miserable.

And Matt and Tori were more unhappy than anyone.

They both blamed themselves and the relationship that had, so quickly, become so important to each of them.

Too important?

The guilt was enough to drive them apart. The only physical contact was the occasional hug—the kind of touch any family member would offer another for comfort and support.

They both knew it was over. This was the fallout they had shelved even thinking about, and it was too huge to be acceptable. The awful truth was not being discussed, however. What was happening with Hayley made anything more personal seem insignificant. Irrelevant.

If…no, *when*…Hayley was returned safely to her family, neither Matt nor Tori would dare risk putting her in danger again. It would be a relief to remove the precipitating factor of their relationship because it might erase some of the guilt they were currently suffering.

The amount that could be erased would never be enough to make it possible to try again, though, would it? Hayley was only the first in a whole line of teenagers that Matt was responsible for steering towards adulthood.

And for Tori, somewhere in that turbulent emotional mix was a kind of relief that the 'I told you so' element had had a real basis. That she should have trusted her instincts. She had every intention of doing so for the rest of her life.

Matt clearly felt the same way and said as much when he finally broke down on the third night after a sobbing Bonnie finally got to sleep.

'The warning was there all along. I was just too selfish to listen.'

'You're not selfish, Matt. You're one of the *least* selfish people I've ever known.'

'Remember that time Hayley got into trouble for swearing at her teacher? I knew that was because I was planning to skive off and have fun for a lousy weekend. I knew how fragile our little family unit was. That day that Jack broke his arm, I said to Mum that they needed time for the emotional dust to settle in their lives.' Matt's snort of laughter was wry. 'I said I wasn't even going to employ a nanny to help because *I* was the only real element of continuity these kids had between their old and new lives.'

'You can't give a hundred per cent of yourself to others all the time, Matt. It's not humanly possible. You have to have some time to yourself.'

'Maybe if it had been time just for myself, it would

have been OK.' Matt shook his head. 'I should have just gone fishing or something. I knew perfectly well how much of a strain it could put on things if I was seen to be lavishing attention on a lover.'

His smile was the saddest Tori had ever seen. 'Why did you have to be so damn irresistible, babe?'

'I never intended it to go this far,' Tori reminded him. 'I had the rules there so clearly—for both of us. There was no way I was going to be a threat to your family because there was no way I was ever going to foster or adopt anyone else's kids.' Utter despair clawed at Tori. 'I should never have suggested we come out of the closet. I thought we were joking when we talked about killing or curing things. It doesn't feel like a joke now, though, does it? I feel like our relationship is dying…or dead already.'

'Maybe we just moved too fast.' Matt's hands touched Tori's and a note of hope touched his voice. 'Maybe we could just turn the clock back a bit and try again.'

'Keep it secret? Bit late for that, Matt.'

'Not keep it secret. Just go back to the way we were, with me coming out to see you whenever I get the chance.'

'A few hours snatched here and there? Ending up in a motel somewhere? Is that what you really want, Matt?'

'Of course it isn't. But do we have a choice?'

'Yes,' Tori said quietly. 'We can make it very clear to everybody that we realise it's not going to work. That's it's completely over. That's the only way Hayley's ever going to feel secure.'

The silence was heartbreaking because Matt obviously couldn't find any way of persuading Tori that she was wrong. Or maybe he didn't want to try because Tori wasn't wrong.

She had known that all along. They were at opposite ends of a spectrum here and they had both known that ever since that awful night when they'd tried to save the teenager who'd died from butane inhalation. Their different standpoints had been crystal clear then.

Matt couldn't not do his best for his nieces and nephews because he couldn't allow them to lose their way, like those teenagers living in the garage had.

Tori couldn't afford to become involved as a pseudo-parent because she knew the kind of emotional damage such efforts could cause. Seeing Monique again had reinforced that vow she'd made all those years ago. How could she have so blithely disregarded all that and accepted Matt's proposal of marriage?

They were both suffering exactly the kind of emotional damage she had known was a possibility. The kind that came from trying to cobble together those pieces that didn't really fit. The kind that could end up distorting the part of the picture that already fitted together well. Their relationship had been bombed by Hayley and it lay in tatters amongst the shards of fear and self-recrimination.

And what of Hayley? What ongoing damage was happening to her? Was she heading for a miserable existence in some squalid garage?

Tori pushed herself heavily to her feet.

'Where are you going?'

'I'll call you later, Matt.' Tori didn't wait to see if Matt was going to stand up and offer her a hug. She really couldn't bear it if he did. 'I've got something I really need to do.'

'OK. I'll call you if we hear anything.'

'Thanks.' Tori didn't make the same promise. The likelihood of her hearing anything first was almost non-existent.

Unless...the hunch she was now following had some kind of a basis. Tori was running on instinct now.

But she had been following her instincts when she had given in to wanting Matt so much, hadn't she? When she had believed they could really make it work? Could they even be trusted any more?

The central city address was easy to remember. Matt had looked it up in records held at the ambulance station and passed it on to the police only two days ago.

'A lot of street kids seem to end up there,' he'd told them. 'Girls about Hayley's age. They live in a garage out behind the house. It'd be worth checking out.'

The police had checked it out and found nothing, but instinct was still drawing Tori there. Monique would be quite likely to refuse any help, but there was a connection there, wasn't there? Someone looking for Hayley from the inside of the subculture of displaced teenagers could well have far more chance of success than someone from the world they were trying to find refuge from.

Monique had been offered help once from Tori's mother, and while she had chosen to reject it, perhaps the memory of the offer would be enough to prompt her to give something back now. It was probably clutching at straws but the desolation on Matt's face tonight would have pushed Tori to try anything that might help.

However farfetched.

However scary it was to approach the dimly lit,

threatening property in a part of town no one should venture alone.

Tori avoided the main house. She did not want to make contact with that tattooed man with the metal spikes under his lips or that older, sullen women who might well take pleasure in retaliating for her intrusion. She trod quietly, skirting the rusty car bodies and stinking piles of household rubbish until she reached the garage.

Months had passed since the dreadful night Charlene had died in this miserable dwelling, but nothing had changed. The single, unshaded bulb still illuminated bare mattresses, floating like islands in a sea of detritus. A strong smell of cannabis masked the more unpleasant odour of filthy bedding and unwashed humanity, and a slight scuffle at one side of the garage advertised the fear that her entrance signalled a raid by authority figures.

'It's all right,' Tori called. She took a quick breath, hoping to steady her voice. 'I'm just a friend of Monique's. Is she around?'

'Nah. Piss off.'

But Tori moved closer instead. One of the girls looked familiar, with her dyed jet-black hair, the heavy make-up and black lipstick. There had been two Goths watching them work on Charlene that night, hadn't there?

'Do you remember me?' Tori asked cautiously. 'I was one of the people that tried to save your friend Charlene.'

The girl shrugged, drawing deeply on the hand-rolled cigarette she held.

'I'm trying to help someone else now. A girl about

your age. But I've run into a dead end. I'm hoping Monique might be able to help me.'

A hunched figure in the small group, with the hood of a sweatshirt pulled forward far enough to shade her face, dropped a cigarette end into the top of an almost empty bottle of vodka. The soft hiss as it was extinguished sounded surprisingly loud.

'Why the hell should I help *you*?' The hood fell back as a head jerked up and was shaken. A head that was partly shaven, with the rest covered in dreadlocked hair.

'Monique!' Tori's smile of relief was genuine. 'Oh, thank goodness you're here.'

'You should go,' Monique told her. 'You don't belong here.'

'Could I just talk to you? Please?'

'What for?'

'I know this girl, Hayley. She's only fifteen.' Tori spoke fast, hoping desperately that Monique would at least take the time to listen. 'She's the niece of a friend of mine, Matt. He was one of the paramedics who tried to save Charlene. Hayley's run away and her family's terribly upset. I thought—'

'The pigs have already been here,' Monique interrupted. 'We don't know anything.'

Tori closed her eyes, fighting back tears of despair. So that was that. Another dead end.

'You're screwing her uncle, aren't you?'

Tori's eyes flew open. There was only one way Monique could sound so sure about that information.

'You *have* seen her,' she gasped. 'You've spoken to Hayley, haven't you? *Please*, Monique—you've got to help me.'

'No, I don't. Why should I?'

'I've got some money.' Tori fished in the back pocket of her jeans and drew out the thin wad of bills she had brought for this purpose. 'You can have it all.'

Crouching down to offer the money, Tori tried to catch Monique's gaze, but it was like touching an eel.

'I'm sorry, Monique,' she said softly. 'I'm sorry I didn't understand anything all those years ago. I'm sorry I didn't try harder to make you feel welcome in my family.'

Painfully thin shoulders moved under the sweatshirt in a shrug. 'Wasn't your fault,' Monique muttered. 'I was a right little bitch back then, anyway.'

It was almost an apology. An acknowledgement that things could have been very different. Tori held her breath as Monique's hand closed over the folded money and dark eyes held hers for a heartbeat.

'She's over there,' Monique said gruffly. 'In bed.'

Hayley lay curled up, concealed by the folds of a dirty blanket. Tori resisted the urge to throw her arms around the girl, crouching and then sitting on the floor beside the mattress instead.

'Are you OK, Hayley?'

'I'm fine.'

She didn't sound fine. 'Are you hungry?'

The silence was an affirmation and Tori felt her own stomach tighten in a sympathetic cramp. 'How 'bout coming out with me to get a hamburger or something?'

'You'd just make me go home.'

Tori could almost believe the statement was, in fact, a request, but she shook her head carefully.

'What would be the point of that? You could always just run away again. Nobody's going to lock you up, Hayley, no matter how much they love you. And, believe me, nobody could love you more than your family does.'

She couldn't be sure in such inadequate light, but the glint in Hayley's eyes could very well have been tears.

'Bonnie's crying herself to sleep every night, Hayley. Charles won't talk to anyone and won't touch his new guitar, and Jack doesn't even smile any more.'

The continued silence felt like encouragement to continue. 'They need their big sister. Don't you think they've been through enough tragedy, losing their mum and dad, without losing you as well?'

'They don't need me. You're going to be their mother.'

'No. That's never going to happen, Hayley.' Tori fought back her own tears when she heard the wobble in the teenager's voice. 'I never intended to be any more than a partner for Matt and a friend to you guys, but even that's not going to happen now.'

'What?'

'Matt made a promise to you and your brothers and sister, Hayley. To love and protect you just as much as your parents would have. He can't keep that promise if I'm around because you've made it very clear that you don't want me around.'

'He loves you more than he loves me.'

'You can't compare different types of love,' Tori said sadly. 'And it doesn't matter anyway, because I love Matt enough to not want to see him get torn apart.'

'What's that supposed to mean?'

'It means that you win, Hayley. I'll get out of your life. Out of Matt's life. On one condition.'

'What's that?'

'That you let me take you home. That you'll stay

there and make an effort to be a real part of your own
family. Maybe it's not the family you had and that's
very sad, but it was nobody's fault—especially not
your fault, and you've got a darned good substitute if
you ask me. You've got an amazing uncle and grandparents and real siblings. It's more than I had.'

Tori had to clear her throat. 'You have people who
love you, Hayley, and they don't even expect you to
love them back. They just want to be able to love you.'

The silence was much longer this time. A heavy, sad
silence. Tori couldn't win here. Her relationship with
Matt couldn't survive, with or without Hayley's presence in the family. The most she could hope for was
to be able to deliver Hayley home safely, but that might
be the last contact she could afford to have with Matt
and that thought was unbearable.

'Could you just, like, drop me at the end of the street
so I could go home by myself?'

'Sure.'

The hesitation was only brief. Maybe it would be
better this way. If Matt didn't know anything about the
promise she'd made to Hayley, he would think she had
dumped him because she couldn't handle the family
situation. He would have every right to be very hurt
and angry, and maybe being that angry would be the
best way to get through the break-up that had to happen. She could just disappear for a few days and the
relief of having Hayley home might make the initial
heartache a lot easier. Matt might even thank her one
day for making the break so clean and clear cut.

Hayley was uncurling herself. She reached for her
jacket, which had been covering a stained, lumpy-
looking pillow.

'Can we stop for that hamburger on the way?'

The take-away meal didn't take long but it was long enough for Tori to say quite a few more things to Hayley. The words of encouragement, advice and even warning probably fell on deaf ears, and the teenager certainly made no response between hurried mouthfuls of food, but in a kind of roundabout way Tori felt she could be making up for the long-ago failure with Monique by offering them.

She let Hayley out at the end of her street, as promised, but she didn't drive away immediately. Her car would be hard to recognise parked amongst others at this distance and, anyway, it was clear that Matt had eyes for nothing other than the person who rang his doorbell.

Tori couldn't see his face but she could read the body language in the hug that lifted Hayley from her feet and then the hold on her arms that kept her just far enough away to confirm that, yes, it really *was* her and that, miraculously, she was unharmed. A very faint sound reached her open car window just before that rectangle of light was extinguished by the closing of the front door.

The sound of laughter. Relieved laughter. Joyous, even.

And Tori made no attempt to check the tears pouring down her face.

However heartbreaking this was, there was no doubt she had done the right thing.

The only thing she could have done for the man she loved.

CHAPTER TEN

IT WASN'T *fair*!

Things were as they should be again. Or, at least, as close to how they should be as it was possible to make them now. But something hadn't worked out quite right and things felt almost as bad as that time after Mum and Dad had been killed in the accident.

Like something really, really bad had happened and life was never going to be the same. Could never be as good. And everyone was trying to be nice to each other and pretend that, in the end, it was all going to be OK and they all knew perfectly well that it wasn't because it couldn't be, could it?

It wasn't supposed to be like this. It just wasn't *fair*.

Uncle Matt was staring off into space again and in the moment of time before he saw her, he looked as though he thought life sucked just as much as Hayley thought so.

'I've finished all my homework, Uncle Matt.'

'Good girl.' The smile looked just the same as it always did, but it didn't get any further than his nose. The lights were off in his eyes.

'Would you like to read my essay? It's about why living in the country is better than living in the city.'

'Sure.'

Hayley watched her uncle as he scanned her work. He'd tell her it was good even if it wasn't, but she had tried really hard. She'd been trying hard all week, dammit. He'd been *so* happy when she'd come home that night. His eyes had danced with lights and he'd even had to brush away tears.

For *her*. He'd cried because he loved her and had been scared about losing her. Nanna had cried as well. And Bonnie. Charles had gone kind of red in the face but Jack had just grinned from ear to ear. They'd all hugged her and called her Haystack, and it had felt so good to feel so wanted.

The good feeling hadn't lasted long, though, had it? She'd had to talk to Uncle Matt about being in the garage and how Tori had come to find her and bring her home, and Matt had looked totally bewildered.

'But where is she now?' he'd asked. 'Why didn't she come in with you?'

And Hayley couldn't tell him she'd only come home because Tori had promised to get out of their lives. She felt too ashamed. As ashamed as she'd been of causing trouble the night her parents had died. Making them late. Making them be in the wrong place at the wrong time when that stupid truck had skidded across the motorway.

Not that anyone blamed her, of course. Or, if they did, it wasn't enough to stop them wanting to have her at home. That part of the plan had worked perfectly. She would always know just how much they really cared. Why couldn't the happiness have lasted longer? Why had it been squashed when Matt had given up even trying to phone Tori within a day or two?

She'd heard him tell Nanna that he'd spoken to her sister, Sarah, and that Tori had gone away for a while to that island they owned in Fiji. He'd looked angry by then. He'd said he couldn't believe she would just walk out on him because of what had happened, and that maybe if she couldn't handle a crisis with the kids then it was probably just as well it hadn't gone any further.

And Nanna had said, 'Don't worry. She's just letting the dust settle. Giving the children time to have you all to themselves. She'll be back.'

But she wouldn't, would she? Tori had made a promise to Hayley that she was going to keep. Later on, when they'd been getting the hamburger, she'd said she could be selfish and try to keep the relationship going, but it would never work. She said that being selfish might get you what you wanted in the short term but she believed that it would come back and bite you in the bum later. 'What goes around, comes around,' she'd said.

That was what was happening here, wasn't it? Hayley wasn't getting what she wanted. None of them were.

Matt handed back the homework. 'It's brilliant, Hayley. Makes me want to go and live in the country. Near a beach and a forest.' He didn't say anything else but they both knew she'd based her essay on Tori's property. Matt cleared his throat. 'Your teachers must be pretty impressed with the way you're working now.'

Hayley shrugged. 'I guess.'

Hazel eyes, so like Mum's had been, were watching her carefully. 'You OK, hon?'

She nodded. 'Sure.'

'You've been pretty quiet all week. You will find someone to talk to if things get bad again, won't you? It doesn't have to be me—I know I'm not hot on teenage girl stuff, but there's Nanna or…or there must be people at school.'

'Counsellors?' Hayley snorted. 'As if! Only losers talk to them.' Who had he been going to suggest in that moment of hesitation? Tori? She'd certainly be a lot more clued up than Nanna. Shopping with her had actually been fun until Hayley had screwed up the nerve to implement the grand plan with the shoplifting bit.

'I'm fine,' Hayley said firmly. She wanted to escape now. Thinking about that shoplifting made her remember something else she'd overheard the adults discussing—that Tori would have to come back for the court appearance soon, and that if she was convicted she'd probably lose her job.

'OK, then.' Matt was still watching her. 'I just don't ever want things to get to the point where you feel you need to run away. Running away is never a good answer.'

Tori had run away. It should have solved things but it hadn't, had it?

'I won't run away again,' Hayley said impatiently. 'I *told* you that. Can't we just forget it?'

'Sure.' The tone was soothing but it made no difference. Hayley was never going to forget the trauma of those mercifully few miserable days. Neither was anyone else, apparently.

Leaving the sitting room, Hayley passed Charles's guitar, propped up in the corner near the door. Abandoned. It even had a layer of dust on it. He'd be in his room now but Hayley didn't want to go in there. He was probably still trying to glue those disgusting bits of rat's bones together.

Bonnie and Jack came out of their bedroom, arguing about something.

'It's mine!'

'No, it's mine! Give it *back*!'

'*No!*'

They pushed past Hayley as Jack chased Bonnie, and the shriek and tears seconds later were inevitable. Hayley waited for Uncle Matt to materialise in the hallway and demand to know what was going on. Then he would sort it out and maybe cart giggling twins off to bed, one under each arm.

But Bonnie just kept sobbing quietly as Jack triumphantly took the prized toy boat into the bathroom and slammed the door.

And Uncle Matt still hadn't appeared.

Hayley's sigh was heartfelt. She crouched in front of Bonnie and gave her an awkward hug.

'I miss Mummy,' Bonnie sobbed.

'I know.' Hayley could feel her own tears prickling and she *never* cried. 'So do I.'

'I miss Tori, too. Why did she have to go away? And you went away. Why does everyone I love have to go away?'

'They don't.' Hayley hugged her little sister harder. 'I'm sorry, Bonnie. I should never have gone away. I won't do it again.'

But Bonnie still sobbed. Hayley hid her own tears in the mop of blonde curls in her arms. 'It's OK, hon,' she whispered. 'Everything's going to be OK, you'll see.'

The rock was a good place to sit.

Solid. Peaceful. The waves were very gentle today and it seemed a lifetime ago that Tori had lain at the base of this rock with her broken leg. All she had to show for that mishap now was a small scar on her shin.

And a much larger scar on her heart.

That holiday that had ended so disastrously had been the first link in the chain, hadn't it? Sarah had been miserable back at home and she herself had been so bored by her enforced inactivity that it had seemed a stroke of genius to drag Sas along to that USAR course. Never mind that Matt had been supposed to have been the perfect man for Sarah.

The USAR link had been what had brought Sarah back to these islands in the wake of that cyclone, and it had ended so much more happily that time with her discovery that Ben was actually her perfect partner.

And that had set Tori up to be ready for the next link. She had been lonely rattling around in that big house by herself, and had then been captured by the excitement of working in that rescue scene with the logging truck MVA. Meeting Matt again and the subsequent friendship had been perfectly timed.

Sarah's wedding had been unfortunately well timed as well. Tori had known Matt long enough to realise how much she liked him, and the setting had been too conducive to finding out how much more she'd wanted from that friendship.

If only she hadn't fallen in love with Matt. If that final link hadn't been added to the chain then it wouldn't be lying there irreparably broken now.

Like her heart.

This pain couldn't last, though, could it? It was already better than it had been a week ago when she had arrived with nothing more than a hastily packed overnight bag. Ben's gardener had brought the boat over to the mainland to fetch her and his wife, Mara had opened the house and cooked a wonderful meal that Tori hadn't been able to summon the appetite to eat.

She hadn't spoken to Matt yet, but she spoke to Sarah every day and knew that life for the Buchanans was getting back to some sort of normal routine. She and Matt would have to talk eventually but it was better to let the dust settle a little first. Matt was upset, of course, but he must be feeling a bit better by now because he hadn't spoken to Sarah or Ben in the last three days.

Sarah was becoming increasingly more concerned with her own state of affairs now. And fair enough—she was two days overdue with the baby and if it didn't start by itself, they were talking about an induction on Friday.

Monday—tomorrow—was the date set for Tori's court appearance on the shoplifting charge.

Going home could not be put off any longer. Her bag was packed. The boat would be waiting for her by the jetty already. Tori stood up, slowly, unaware of her soft sigh as she turned her back on the beach and started walking back to reality.

Sarah was there to meet her at the airport, as promised.

It was a grey day, which suited Tori's mood perfectly, but the clouds were breaking by the time they got north of the harbour bridge and the late afternoon sun was shining strongly when Sarah steered her car between the worst of the ruts in Tori's driveway.

'Are you sure you should be still driving? Those potholes could set off labour, you know.'

'I wish.' Sarah pulled on the handbrake and groaned. 'I just want to get it over with now. I'm sick of the waiting. I keep getting Braxton-Hicks' contractions and thinking, Hooray, this is *it*. But they're never the real thing.'

'Are you coming in for a cup of tea?'

'In a minute. There's someone who wants a word with you first.'

Tori could feel herself going pale. 'Matt's not here, is he? Oh, my God, I'm not ready for this, Sas. How could you not tell me?'

'It's not Matt who wants the talk.' Sarah's smile was reassuring. 'It's something about that court appearance tomorrow, and I was told it needed to be private.'

'Oh.' Tori's nod was grim. 'Right. I'll come and get you in a minute or two, then. Wish me luck?'

Sarah smiled again. 'Don't think you'll need it somehow.'

Turning the corner, Tori was astonished to find Hayley sitting on the top of the steps leading to her verandah.

'Hi, Tori.' A quick glance came her way before it was screened as the teenager's head ducked, swinging the length of straight, mousy hair forward as a shield.

'Hi.' Tori climbed the steps somewhat cautiously. It felt awkward, standing there looking down at the bent head, so she sat beside Hayley on the step. 'Did you want to talk to me?'

'Yeah. I…ah…wanted to say sorry.'

'Oh…' It was only one word but it said rather a lot. 'Thanks, Hayley.'

'I went to see the police,' Hayley continued. 'And that shopkeeper. I explained what had really happened.' She caught Tori's gaze and held it a little longer this time. 'They've dropped that charge against you. You don't have to go to court tomorrow.'

'Really?' Relief and delight warred with disbelief. Was Hayley winding her up for some reason? But there was something different about this girl sitting beside her. It took a long moment for Tori to realise what it was.

'You've grown up, Hayley,' she said in surprise. 'How did you manage that in the space of a week?'

The shrug was pure teenager. Defiant and insecure all at the same time. 'Guess I've had a lot to think about.'

'We all have,' Tori sighed. 'Hasn't been much fun, has it?'

'That's for sure.'

The silence was punctuated by the tiny bird that darted in to land on a branch of the wisteria framing the verandah posts. The delicious kissing squeaks of the friendly fantail coaxed a poignant smile from Tori.

'I haven't lost everything, then,' she murmured. 'I'll be able to get back to work without worrying about being fired.' She moved to stand up but Hayley's face jerked towards her.

'Wait!' Hayley was chewing her bottom lip, a picture of anxiety. 'I…I talked to Uncle Matt as well.'

Tori sank back onto the step and silently did as she had been requested. She waited.

'He was kind of mad at you, you know? He thought you'd walked out on him because we were all too much trouble. I…I told him about the promise you'd made so that I'd go home. And…' Hayley's voice dropped. 'I told him what you'd said about loving him enough to stay away even if it wasn't what *you* wanted.'

Tori's heart was thumping painfully. 'What did *he* say?'

Hayley didn't answer. Instead, she got to her feet. 'There's something I want to show you,' she said. 'Inside.'

It was hard to get her head around what was happening here. Tori followed Hayley into her own house and her bewilderment increased as Hayley headed towards the little-used, huge, formal lounge of the house.

Bonnie was standing outside the door. She was wearing a blue dress and had some white daisies poked amongst the curls of her blonde hair. She was managing to look both excited and nervous and she held the hand of a much smaller girl.

Phoebe was wearing her flower girl dress from Sarah's wedding. She was also carrying the same basket she had held at that ceremony, but the petals it contained were far less exotic than island blooms. Tori noted that the iceberg roses from her garden must be minus a fair few flowers.

She shook her head at the irrelevant thought. 'What on earth is going on?' she asked.

'You'll see.' The voice came from behind and Tori's head swivelled to find Sarah grinning at her. 'Excuse me, but I need to go inside first. I'm a guest here.'

Tori's jaw dropped as the door opened to admit Sarah. She could see that the furniture in the room had been totally rearranged. There were two rows of chairs and people were sitting there. All dressed up. Linda was wearing a large pink hat!

The white rhododendrons, which would be at their best in the garden right now, must be even balder than the roses, Tori thought distractedly. Their blooms seemed to be everywhere in the room and the soft scent filled the silence.

Except that it wasn't silent any longer. From one side of the room came some clear, if rather inexpert notes, plucked by a boy passionate about classical guitar music.

Jack was standing on a box at the end of the aisle formed by armchairs, a book open in his hands. And standing in front of Jack, with his head turned and a sheepish grin on his face…was Matt. Wearing a suit. Holding a bunch of daisies that looked a tiny bit wilted, like the ones in Bonnie's hair.

Tori was completely stunned. This was obviously intended to be a wedding.

Her wedding.

Bonnie bent down and whispered in Phoebe's ear. Phoebe giggled and took a huge handful of rose petals from her basket, throwing them in front of her with a delightful enthusiasm. Bonnie walked after her and when the second handful of petals had been scattered, Hayley nudged Tori.

'You go next,' she whispered. 'I walk behind you.'

Tori took a step obediently but then stopped. 'I don't understand,' she whispered back.

'It's a practice,' Hayley said softly. 'For the real thing. We want you to marry Uncle Matt, Tori. Please?'

What could she do? The faces of the 'guests'—Bob and Linda Buchanan, and Ben and Sarah Dawson— were expectant. Encouraging. Phoebe was still hurling rose petals everywhere and Bonnie was helping. Charles was starting his song for the third time and Jack was trying to stand still and look serious but was in some danger of falling off the box as he shifted impatiently from foot to foot.

And Matt. Matt was just looking as though Tori was the only person on earth that he had eyes for. The force of love in that gaze drew Tori forward irresistibly. How could she not move closer when her own love for this man was equally magnetic?

He gave her the bunch of daisies. He gave her his

heart in the gaze that locked with her own and Tori had to blink back sudden tears.

'I'm not really dressed for this,' she whispered.

Matt simply smiled. He winked at Jack.

'Dearly…'

'Beloved,' Hayley prompted from her position to one side of Tori.

'Beloved.' Jack raised his voice to something close to a shout. 'We are gathered…' He looked down at the sheet of paper which the book in his hands was concealing. 'Together to ask something special. Uncle Matt, do—'

'No,' Hayley said. 'Full names, remember?'

'Oh…right.' Jack squared his shoulders. 'Matthew Charles Buchanan, do you want to marry Tori?'

'Yes,' Matt said solemnly. 'I sure do.'

'And Tor—'

'Victoria,' Hayley supplied.

'Oh, yes. Victoria Anne Preston. Do you want to marry Uncle Matt?'

'Yes.' Tori had to scrub away an errant tear. She found her hand caught and squeezed by Matt. 'Of course I do.'

'Right.' Jack gazed around the room. Does anybody here have any reason why these two people can't get married? Speak now or forever hold your tongue.'

'Peace,' Hayley corrected softly.

'Please,' Jack added loudly with a satisfied nod.

A faint ripple of amusement came from the watching guests and then Jack took a deep breath.

'Does anybody here have any reason why these two people *should* get married? Speak now, or forever—'

'I do.' Ben was grinning broadly as he interrupted.

'I'd really like to have Matt for a brother-in-law and Phoebe's pretty keen on getting a bunch of cousins.'

'I'd love to see this house full of a family,' Sarah added. 'And…and I want to see my sister with the man who loves her as much as I know Matt does.'

'I want to see my son with the woman who's perfect for *him*,' Linda said. 'Someone with a spirit sunny enough for any number of people planets to orbit.' She reddened as Bob cleared his throat in embarrassment at her awful metaphor. 'Sorry. It must be that project on astronomy the twins started this week.' She nudged Bob.

'It's about time something really happy happened in this family,' he said gruffly. 'And I hope you two are as happy as Linda and I have always been.'

Charles had gone very red. 'I like Tori,' he mumbled. 'It'd be cool if she came to live with us.'

Jack nodded. 'Uncle Matt's been kind of sad with you gone,' he informed Tori. 'We all have.'

Bonnie gazed up at Tori. 'I love you, too, Tori, and I really want you to be…' She paused to glare at Hayley defiantly. 'I know I'm not supposed to say it but I'm still little and I *need* a mummy. Phoebe's got Sarah now and I…I want Tori.'

A small body edged closer and Tori put her arm around Bonnie and smiled down at the tear-filled blue eyes.

Hayley wasn't smiling. 'I've been an ass,' she said bluntly. 'You might not believe me, Tori, but a lot of what you said made sense. You get back what you give and I really want my family to be happy again. I know I've made it seem like it's going to be horrible and difficult, but we'll try to help and we do all want you in…as a…' Hayley sighed, unable to find the right words. Then she shrugged, her speech clearly abandoned.

Matt's hold on Tori's hand tightened. The silence, as he collected the words he wanted, felt as though a collective breath was being held by everyone present in this room.

Including Tori.

And then Matt spoke.

'Life hasn't been the same without you around,' he told her softly. 'It could never be the same. Love is like magic dust, isn't it? I love these kids and that sprinkles some around, but loving you sprinkles even more and so we all get the benefit. I could never love another woman as much as I love you, Victoria Preston.' Matt paused again and swallowed and then he smiled apologetically. 'I'll think up some much better vows for the real thing, I promise.'

'No need.' Tori smiled back. 'As far as I'm concerned, Matthew Buchanan, this has been as real as it needs to be. I love you, too. I want to spend the rest of my life with you and I'm happy to share that life with your whole family.' She turned to grin at Sarah. 'I'm collecting more additions to mine all the time. It's just as well we've got a nice, big house for Christmas dinners, isn't it?'

Sarah groaned. Loudly. And it clearly wasn't the thought of cooking Christmas dinner for such a large family that was causing her distress.

'Oh, my God!' Tori stared at her sister. 'Are you...'

Ben was on his feet. Matt turned and started moving, still hanging on to Tori's hand. Sarah clutched at her swollen belly, waited for the contraction to subside, and then smiled shakily at the anxious faces surrounding her.

'I think this is the real thing,' she warned.

Tori smiled at the look she caught in Matt's eyes. There was no doubt about it, was there?

'It sure is,' she murmured.

The luxury of confirming their love for each other would have to wait, however. Ben was looking decidedly pale.

'What's the hold-up here? Has someone called for an ambulance yet?'

Introducing a very special holiday collection

Inside you'll find

Roses for Christmas *by Betty Neels*

Eleanor finds herself working with the forceful Fulk van
Hensum from her childhood – and sees that he hasn't
changed. So why does his engagement to another woman
upset her so much?

Once Burned *by Margaret Way*

Celine Langton ends her relationship with Guy Harcourt
thinking he deserves someone more sophisticated. But why
can't she give back his ring?

A Suitable Husband *by Jessica Steele*

When Jermaine begins working with Lukas Tavinor,
she realises he's the kind of man she's always dreamed of
marrying. Does it matter that her sister feels the same way?

On sale Friday 7th October 2005

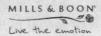

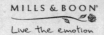

researching the cure

The facts you need to know:

- **One woman in nine** in the United Kingdom will develop breast cancer during her lifetime.

- Each year **40,700** women are newly diagnosed with breast cancer and around **12,800** women will die from the disease. However, survival rates are improving, with on average 77 per cent of women still alive five years later.

- **Men can also suffer from breast cancer**, although currently they make up less than one per cent of all new cases of the disease.

Britain has one of the highest breast cancer death rates in the world. Breast Cancer Campaign wants to understand why and do something about it. Statistics cannot begin to describe the impact that breast cancer has on the lives of those women who are affected by it and on their families and friends.

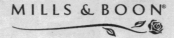

**During the month of October
Harlequin Mills & Boon will donate
10p from the sale of every
Modern Romance™ series book to
help Breast Cancer Campaign
in *researching the cure.***

Breast Cancer Campaign's scientific projects
look at improving diagnosis and treatment
of breast cancer, better understanding how
it develops and ultimately either curing the
disease or preventing it.

Do your part to help

Visit www.breastcancercampaign.org

And make a donation today.

researching the cure

Breast Cancer Campaign is a company limited by guarantee registered in England and Wales. Company No. 05074725. Charity registration No. 299758.

FREE!

4 Books
and a surprise gift!

We would like to take this opportunity to thank you for reading this Mills & Boon® book by offering you the chance to take FOUR more specially selected titles from the Medical Romance™ series absolutely FREE! We're also making this offer to introduce you to the benefits of the Reader Service™—

- ★ **FREE home delivery**
- ★ **FREE gifts and competitions**
- ★ **FREE monthly Newsletter**
- ★ **Exclusive Reader Service offers**
- ★ **Books available before they're in the shops**

Accepting these FREE books and gift places you under no obligation to buy, you may cancel at any time, even after receiving your free shipment. Simply complete your details below and return the entire page to the address below. You don't even need a stamp!

YES! Please send me 4 free Medical Romance books and a surprise gift. I understand that unless you hear from me, I will receive 6 superb new titles every month for just £2.75 each, postage and packing free. I am under no obligation to purchase any books and may cancel my subscription at any time. The free books and gift will be mine to keep in any case.

M5ZEF

Ms/Mrs/Miss/Mr ....Initials................................
BLOCK CAPITALS PLEASE

Surname ....

Address ....

....

....Postcode ....

Send this whole page to:
UK: FREEPOST CN81, Croydon, CR9 3WZ